DEVIOUSLY DELICIOUS

A Jills of All Trades Mystery (Book One)

T.J. DESCHAMPS

BETH WHITEMAN

Edited by

EMILY PAPER

Edited by

PATRICIA LONG

To all those who want to escape in a story, at least for a little while.

DEVIOUSLY DELICIOUS

PROLOGUE

I walked to keep an eye on things. You could never tell when things would go wrong, so every day I made sure they were still all right. Or as right as they could be with everyone living so far from where they belonged.

The walk always started along the bay, as that is where I made my home in a small, square, drab building that no one would notice, hiding in the open. The walks were pleasant enough, interesting enough. A pretty little view. One of the reasons I chose this town was the view. There was not an ocean where I came from, and if I had to live away from home, it may as well have been somewhere with a pretty little view. This world was not as green, would never have the magic of home, but it worked for now. Had been working for years.

This walk was different. It was not pleasant; the view did not hold any interest. This walk wasn't because I needed to make sure something wouldn't go wrong, but because something had.

One of them out there had something that was mine, and I needed it back. They were out there with my possession, my key.

Mrs. Hubbard, an elderly woman with more dogs than sense and never a spare dime, stood on the front porch of her bungalow, smoking. She tilted her chin when she saw me, stubbornly holding her head high. I knew she was not the one holding what was mine. She wasn't important enough, not a big enough name. She was an entry in a compilation, not a main character. Still, I held her eyes until she looked away, down to one of the hounds that sat at her feet. The dogs whined as I passed by, nervously shifting around the old woman, each one skinnier than the next. It was a wonder none of them had ever starved.

Past the bay, with its businesses and busyness, past people who weren't relevant to my story, there was one of the families, the charming father and the beautiful mother, their children. They should be perfectly happy. What wasn't there to be happy about? I made this world so it would be so. But instead, suspicion lurked in the eyes of the parents, fear in the kids. I was there when those children were born. I touched their minds, gifting them a chance to have a perfect life, to have *any* life at all. There shouldn't be suspicion or fear. There should only be the blissful images of a life well lived.

Three more families along the way. All fearful.

They each watched me as I passed, slowly trekking through the town I claimed. *For them.* Whether they knew it or not. I erased it all, of course. Their before lives. I had to if I wanted to keep them safe. I had to do it. And now they watched me with their suspicions. As if I was the cause of their concern.

But it wasn't me who made this trouble. Someone out there had something of mine. They're the ones who should be watched.

I walked. Spent my whole morning making the rounds, contacting every one of my people, one way or another. The working men before they headed to their labor. The mothers with their babes. The girls and their enamored boys, all playing at a life that was never supposed to be. I watched and I walked, and I searched for what was taken from me. It must be found and soon. Before the fool who held it realized what it was capable of and ruined not just this life I'd given them, but any life at all.

Chapter One

CHAMPAGNE AND CAVIAR TASTE ON A CHEESE AND CRACKER BUDGET

The palace towered before them, massive and imposing. It served as a symbol of all that was wrong in this world. Allison meant to burn it down or tear it apart with her bare hands, if necessary. She held her blade in a swordswoman stance. Her fellow rebels flanked her left and right, ready to fight the royal guard. Beside her were a hodgepodge of immigrants, factory workers, and craftspeople. Commoners.

Some might have rebelled against the unfair taxes. Others against the oppressive laws that choked the joy out of life here. No, those hardships seemed almost bearable. All of them could no longer stomach the cruelty of their capricious ruler. At the queen's whim, the blood of their kinfolk had whetted the executioner's blade of the palace before them for far too long. Lifeless faces stared back at them from pikes. A reminder of what would happen if the rebels failed.

"This victory will be for the people. No more monarchs. No more tyranny!"

The palace gates opened, vomiting knights in rows of two. Rectangular shields with the crest of the queendom in one hand. Swords at the ready in the other. Many would die at the tip of those blades. Wasn't it better to die free and fighting than rotting in one of her oubliettes?

"Hey. We should stop the campaign here and save our progress. This battle might take a few tries before we get to the boss, and I got an early morning at work," a deep male voice came over her headphones, jerking Allison out of the moment like a needle scratch on a record.

The tower shrank to mere inches tall on a flat screen. Three monitors, a glowing mic, and a mouse rose around it. Shelves with bobble heads, figurines, plushies, and books replaced the vaguely European city. No one flanked her sides. She was in her room, alone again. Yet, the rebels were all protesting in her earphones.

Allison puffed out her breath, exasperated. Not only had she been caught up in her player's head, but she was also live streaming. Her viewers would be pissed off for cutting off gameplay at a crucial moment. The thing was, she wasn't making that much from the livestreams, and she had a day job to go to in the morning as well. "Fine, Mr. Purrkins."

"Thanks, WanderGirl."

"No prob. We'll discuss times that work for everyone in the group chat."

"Be safe out there. Another kid went missing."

Her heart skipped a beat. *I gotta get out of this damned town.*

"Will do. Night folx!"

As her online friends logged off, she flashed a smile at her webcam.

"Thanks for watching my livestream. Give a poor girl a boon and hit that coin button until your finger goes numb. Don't forget to smash that subscribe button when you're done." She blew kisses at the mic. In her peripheral, she looked at the 'coins' she'd collected from streaming go up. After the company that hosted the streaming service got their cut, she might have enough to pay her credit card down this month. At this rate, she'd never get out of Sueños del Mar.

Her eyes snagged on her face on the screen. A woman with silver blonde hair in space buns wearing pink, cat ear headphones looked back at her with bright green irises—admittedly shadows of sleep deprivation smudged under her eyes. A memory of the bruises that had once been there flashed. There and gone. No. She'd never have that happen again. She was making sure of it.

Ideally, she'd shut off the camera, change out of her t-shirt into comfy pajamas, and wash off her makeup, but her subscribers would keep paying as long as she left the camera on. It wouldn't be the first time she'd let strangers watch her sleep for virtual coins that turned into real cash in her account. She got as comfy as possible in her gaming chair and fell asleep.

~

*A*llison bit her lip as her hand hovered over the mouse. The heels cost as much as her half of the rent, but the pumps were covered in Strass crystals and the suede interior promised to be soft as kitten fur. The shoes paired with the vintage dress she snagged from the thrift store bin and the D&G sunglasses. She would get a yacht club date and a man that would get her out of this town.

"Bye bye, Sueños Del Mar," she murmured, clicking on the checkout. Her heart raced as adrenaline pumped through her veins. The plan would work. She'd get out and see the freaking world ... and leave her damned past in this podunk town.

A firm knock, three times, pulled her out of her reverie. Her housemate Dee's voice came through the door. "Our first job is at 8 a.m., and I took on an extra client this afternoon."

"Let me get changed real quick!"

Allison blew a quick kiss to her webcam before closing out the screens, shutting everything down. Yeah. Her subscribers watched her just looking at a screen, too. She live-streamed clipping her cat's claws once and still earned.

She quickly changed out of her regular clothes to her pink polo and jeans she'd wear to work.

Rabbit, her cat, rose from his fluffy bed and stretched, purring. She stopped to give him a pet on his hairless head and then scooped him into her arms.

Dee waited in the hall. Her dark auburn hair was neatly plaited away from her face. She wore overalls over their agreed upon pink polo shirts with their company logo for Jill of All Trades. Their business cards read: Cleaning, Handiwork, Furniture Repair, and Pet Sitting.

Her friend waxed an apologetic smile. "Sorry to add another job. It was some sort of emergency. They had a break-in and don't feel safe returning to their house the way the criminals left it."

"A break-in?" Allison rubbed her arms for warmth. "First a couple of kids go missing and now this. I thought Sueños Del Mar was boring but at least it *was* safe."

A niggling voice whispered, *It was never safe for you.* She blocked the voice out. No need to think about that now.

Worry etched lines onto Dee's normally smooth forehead, as she wrung her hands. "That's the thing. Their kids were the two who were taken a few days ago. We gotta make it look like nothing happened so they can feel safe in their own home."

"Gotcha." It was a miracle she could be so nonchalant when inside, she quaked with fear. *What if this person realized there were two twenty-somethings living without any protection but a dog and a cat?*

Allison cuddled Rabbit closer as the two of them made their way downstairs.

The house was built soon after the gold rush years and had the weight of history and prior occupants to it. Allison loved lines of architecture, the craftsmanship of the woodwork, the stained glass. One didn't see this level of detail in new builds. They were all clean lines, cold, and lacking personality. That's the one thing she loved about her small town: the buildings had character. She didn't love it enough to stay, but she did love the aesthetic.

The roommates' furniture was secondhand, thrifted or from a garage sale. They refinished each piece themselves. Restoring antique furniture was part of their business.

While Dee wrangled her Doberman, Kansas, into his crate, Allison padded to the kitchen. She fed Rabbit some wet food with gravy. While she rinsed out the can and tossed it in the recycling, the cat lapped at his food.

She thought about how Mr. Purrrkins had a velvet voice. He always talked about going into work. Maybe he was some sort of New York lawyer or stockbroker, on his way to making it rich. Did he watch her streams? Did he know what she looked like? *Maybe he was a narcissistic twat that would lay hands on me the first time I did something he didn't like.*

She needed to get out of this town, or she'd keep thinking this way.

Dee appeared in the kitchen, leaned against the wainscoting of the doorframe and folded her arms across her chest. "I'm ready when you are, Allie."

She bristled. Even though they were about the same age, Dee could be a little too mother hen about punctuality and schedule following. So, what if Allison sometimes drifted into daydreams and dawdled? Sometimes that's all a girl had in the daily grind of manual labor. She blew off her annoyance and grabbed the keys from the rack next to the back door.

"I'm driving."

A 1965 Ford F100, Dee and Allison had dubbed Bertha, lived in an old carriage house out back. Her cherry red paint, the metal body, her chrome work, and her lines all spoke of a time when things were made for an aesthetic over function. The truck got about ten miles to a gallon—not business savvy in that aspect, but Sueños Del Mar was a small town, and they never got jobs outside of the city. Also, Bertha was absolutely free and still under Dee's uncle's insurance. Uncle Hank technically owned Bertha, but they'd borrowed her for about fifteen years.

All Uncle Hank asked in return was that they kept her in good shape. Dee and Allison did most of her body work maintenance themselves, but they outsourced the engine work.

Allison slid on her D&G sunglasses and put the old-fashioned key in the ignition. She and Dee held their breath. With a truck this old, it could break down at any time. Bertha started with only a slight hitch. The engine was loud and vibrated the bench seat, but there weren't any telltale clunks, clinks, or stutters of trouble.

They let out a collective sigh of relief.

"Do we have time for Black Forest Bakery?"

Dee grinned at her. "We always have time for Black Forest Bakery."

Five minutes later they pulled in front of the shop. The exterior had a wooden sign that looked like a Black Forest cake with cream filling and cherries on top. The glass front of the shop had all kinds of baked treats painted on the glass as well as the name of the bakery in fancy gold lettering. The place made her gleeful as a child every time she saw it.

When they walked in the door, a bell chimed. The sound accompanied the aroma of freshly baked cakes, pies, cookies, and all manner of desserts enveloped her.

She closed her eyes and moaned. "It smells so good in here."

"I bought a new cologne. Glad you like it." The kind of deep, velvety voice made for radio crooned. A hint of a teasing laced his tone. The voice seemed so familiar.

Allison opened her eyes, hoping for a man in a business suit that was ready to take her far, far away from here. No such luck. Mrs. Leckermaul's assistant, whatever his name was, stood behind the counter.

Dee examined the pastries on display. "Where's Mrs. Leckermaul?"

She might as well have asked a statue. The clerk's focus, his smile was all for Allison as if they had a long acquaintance. As if they knew each other's innermost secrets. My god, that smile! It was so enticing, she almost found herself smiling back.

Yes. He had cool hair, dark brown that emphasized his amber eyes. Yes. He had nice lips. Yes. He had well-defined arms with interesting tattoos. Yes. He could easily make a lot of money on social media simply baking and flexing for thirst traps, but, no, she would not smile back at him. Her taste in men sucked. If it wasn't transactional, she didn't want it.

Besides, the clerk had the kind of grin that suggested he knew something you didn't. It likely got him a lot of phone numbers when he flashed that ridiculously perfect set of teeth to most women, but it perturbed her. She didn't like when people knew things she didn't. She also didn't trust men that could have anyone. They usually had a bad side, and *that* was worse than being poor.

Allison wrinkled her nose and shot him a baleful look. "I meant the pastries."

He ignored her disdain. "Lemme guess. Two strudels: One raspberry and one blueberry."

How did he know? Was he one of her fans? She readied herself to deny any sort of affiliation with WanderGirl.

However, he simply waited for her confirmation.

"Yes. Add a brötchen for my lunch... Please."

"Anything else you desire, ma'am?"

Something unfamiliar coiled inside her. Something she quashed long ago. Believing it better to focus on the ideal life than the ideal love life.

Allie shrugged a shoulder and eyed the treats. There were a lot more in the case than usual. Her stomach rumbled. She peered at the clerk through her eyelashes. He was fixated on her but didn't seem to have heard her mutinous stomach.

"That'll be all."

"As the lady wishes." He bowed with a flourish.

She snorted.

Dee cleared her throat and waved her hand. "Hey. Over here! I'd like to order, too."

The clerk dragged his amber eyes off Allison and focused them on Dee. The smile dimmed to professional courtesy. Not, rude but not overtly flirtatious either. "Yes. Of course. What can I get you?"

Something in Allison softened to that.

Dee folded her arms and looked at the selection in the glass case. "Hard to decide. Looks like you were a busy bee this morning. I've never seen this much selection, and it all seems scrumptious."

The clerk shook his head and held up his hands. "I wish I could take the credit for the stock, but Mrs. Leckermaul was in here early, baking up a storm. She's even making the deliveries today. Normally, that's my job." His gaze swept over to Allison again. When his eyes met hers, the smile reappeared. "That's why you're stuck with me."

"Deliveries! Isn't Mrs. Leckermaul eighty or ninety?" Dee asked, her tone incredulous, adding, "I'll have an apple strudel."

"Beats me." He donned a pair of gloves, grabbed a to-go bag and tongs from their respective holders, and then opened the glass case filled with goodies. Before he ducked to select a pastry, he added, "She usually acts like she's about that old, but lately she's been—" He paused as if searching for the right word. "—sprier. Today, she looked like she had some work done on her face, but that's unlikely. She's a no-nonsense woman."

"Maybe she was going through a rough patch?" Allison suggested, agreeing that Mrs. Leckermaul was all business whenever she came in. A woman who wouldn't engage in small talk didn't care what people thought of her personal appearance. She was always clean and neat but never made up, and surely not the type to get any sort of fillers, Botox, or a face lift.

Dee frowned the way she did when something didn't add up but made no comment.

"An old lady looking younger isn't the most bizarre thing around Sueños del Mar, unfortunately," the clerk said as he bagged their pastries. "Did you hear that they found one of the missing children? Kid was completely unharmed, but fast asleep. Doctors are saying he won't wake up." His gaze again landed on Allison. "Be careful out there."

An icy frisson clambered up Allie's spine, reminding her of another person who never woke up and eventually died. She shook that unbidden memory away. "That's awful."

Dee cleared her throat. "I heard that another kid was found the same way."

The clerk glanced at the redhead as if seeing her for the first time even though they'd just spoken. "Hadn't heard that. You sure?"

Allison put an arm around the now wilting Dee. "Yup. If she says it. Then it's true. My friend pays a lot more attention to what's going on around here than most people. I don't have to bother reading or watching the news at all."

"Good friend to have," he said, bagging up Allison's pastries separately and with more care than he had with Dee's. "It doesn't hurt to stay informed."

The clerk rang up Dee's pastries first, and she paid. Allison reached into her purse, pulling out her credit card. She bit her lip, hoping the shoes didn't set her over her limit.

The clerk held the bag out with a wide grin on his handsome face. His other hand waved her card away. "Don't bother. It's on me."

Her stupid heart stuttered, and a wave of gratitude hit her before suspicion set in. She narrowed her eyes. "Why?"

The grin reached all the way to his eyes. The amber irises danced with something wild and tempting. "Because you're a pretty lady, and I want to buy you a treat."

"Thanks." She took the bag hastily, ignoring the way his fingers brushed hers, and the electric spark dancing up her arm from his touch. She rushed out with her friend.

In the truck, Dee said, "If you take free stuff from him, he's going to expect a date at some point."

Allie took a bite out of her bread before starting the truck. "He can expect all he wants. It'll take more than some strudel to get a date with me." If he bought her a first-class ticket to Europe, on the other hand...

"Ah yes. Champagne and caviar taste doesn't go well with a cheese and cracker budget... It's strange about Mrs. Leckermaul though," Dee mused. "I thought that old lady was on her way out."

It was strange. This town sometimes was. Unlike the kids disappearing and reappearing in a coma, Allison passed off Mrs. Leckermaul's transformation to California Weird.

"Maybe she got a plastic surgeon boyfriend?"

Dee opened her pastry bag. "Or a girlfriend."

"Point."

"Soooo, you're totally not interested? I know he's not your type, but I thought I saw something between y—"

Allison cut her off. "Not interested."

Not after I invested in those shoes to get a yacht club date, she didn't add. He might have paid for breakfast, but a baker couldn't afford a yacht club date, let alone a yacht club life. She would not give up her dream of leaving Sueños Del Mar, of seeing the world, even if he had a smile that made her knees weak.

Chapter Two

WISHES AND DREAMS

rs. Leckermaul was magic. Had to be. There was no other way to explain how every bite of Dee's apple strudel was better than the one before. And, if the appreciative moans coming from the driver's seat were any indication, Allie thought so, too. It was good they had a few moments to enjoy delicious breakfast treats, because this day was going to be hard. Which was, of course, her own doing. Taking on more than she should was practically Dee's *modus operandi*. However, dragging Allie along with her wasn't. The guilt was already pecking at her.

Although cleaning houses was not what either of them imagined when they decided to create Jill of All Trades, it somehow managed to encompass the vast majority of their jobs. Jobs she—Dorseigh Marie MacHale—accepted on behalf of their company. So, if anyone were to blame, it was her. She may as well take the blame, anyway. If there was any guilt to be had, she would gladly carry it. Well, maybe not *gladly*, but she took it on. Guilt and anxiety were basically her best friends.

"You're scowling," Allie said, smacking her arm with a sticky hand. "Ew. Gross. Sorry. Do you have a wet wipe over there, grandma?"

Dee didn't, but the truck did, because she'd put a travel package inside the small glove box only last week, when, she could point out, Allie had snickered at her for it.

"What?" She asked innocently, balancing the last few bites of strudel on her knee to open the glove box and pass a few wipes to Allie. "Did the baker not give you napkins? I'm surprised, because the way he was looking at you, you probably could have gotten him to give you his shirt."

Allie's eyes narrowed, a finger tapping the steering wheel as she waited at a stop to make the turn into the upper-class neighborhood where their first job waited. "We have established that I have no interest in a baker's assistant. To be fair, he should take off whatever it was he was wearing this morning. Did you see it? Some horrendous poly-blend, I bet." She shuddered.

An unexpected laugh escaped Dee. She shoved the last of the strudel into her mouth to keep it from turning into an absolute guffaw. Sometimes her laughs got away from her. "I don't know. I bet he's even prettier without a shirt on," she sputtered around the sugary pastry.

"What was up with him, anyway? Who flirts with customers at a *bakery*? Can you imagine what sorts of delusions he must be living under to think he should flirt with me?" Allie easily maneuvered the truck in between a a pristine Genesis and a rusted-out Pontiac that most likely belonged to the friend of someone's kid or a visiting cousin. The Splatz's neighborhood did not tolerate rusty eyesores. Allie performed the perfect parallel parking job exactly one house away from where they were headed. It probably went without saying, but Allie was braver than Dee in all ways. Never in a million years would Dee have attempted to parallel park within a block of a Genesis. She imagined the bill she'd receive for even nicking the paint could bankrupt her for life.

"You're right. How dare he?" She rolled her eyes at her friend's snobbery. She got it though. Allison was not secretive about her goals. "I've seen him around, you know. He seemed okay, not a total schlub. I think I saw him last week at..." She willed the memory to come, but instead it flickered in her mind, staticky and unfocused. "I can't remember. But I definitely have seen him around. Anyway." She crumbled up her wipe and the wax paper the strudel was wrapped in, cramming them into the white bakery bag. "Let's get this over with."

"Wait." Allie's hand clamped on her arm, nodding towards the white-haired man shuffling up the street. "How is he everywhere? It's so bizarre. What's with all the weirdos this morning? Are they all out?"

Dee wasn't sure she agreed with Allie's assessment of the bakery assistant, but the old man was certainly odd. He was the town eccentric in a town full of eccentrics. Eccentric in that he did seem to be everywhere and knew everyone, even if Dee had not found one person who knew the old man's name. Nor where he lived. Nor what he did when he wasn't walking Sueños Del Mar's sidewalks.

"Leander says he's harmless."

"Leander is as big as a house. Everyone is harmless to him."

Dee's cheeks heated. Dee's cheeks always heated at the mere mention of Leander Mann. She wished she hadn't braided her hair, so she'd have something to hide behind. Luckily, Allie wasn't looking at her, focused instead on the old man.

He nodded at them, a placid, thin-lipped smile on his face, faded blue eyes bouncing over Bertha, the logo on her door, the gear in her bed, and then back to Allison and Dorseigh before shuffling on down the sidewalk.

"So weird."

"Must be why you see him all over the place," Dee teased, opening her door. "You attract weirdos like moths to flames."

"Ha," Allie shouted as Dee slammed the door. "It's better than you and all your needy freaks."

"I do not have needy freaks. What are you even talking about?"

Sadly, she did not need her roommate and friend to expand on the comment. Somehow, she'd developed a reputation as a fixer. Which, considering their business, could be a good thing. Unfortunately, people migrated to her for other sorts of fixes. Positive reinforcement, praise, an ear to listen, a shoulder to cry on. They wanted someone who dropped everything and ran to help, no matter the issue. Helping their neighbor with his garden, the farmer on the edge of town whenever his dog ran off, the junkyard guy with his inventory program, Leander whenever he needed his shop watched for an afternoon. It didn't matter. When someone needed help, she would lend them whatever it was they needed.

Come to think of it, maybe her reputation was less "fixer" and more "sucker."

"Like you said, let's get this over with," Allie grunted, hefting an ancient Filter Queen vacuum from the truck bed. Sure, the thing was as old as the towering redwoods at the edge of town and nearly as heavy, plus it broke down every other week, but it was the best vacuum cleaner she'd ever had and a testament to their skill that they kept it running. "Cleaning up after the Splatz party this morning, right, and remind me what's next?"

"Cleaning up the crime scene from where the two kids were taken." Dee said absently, staring down the street where the old man had disappeared. This would be the first time they had been used for a crime-scene cleanup. "I guess they put up a fight. Holes in walls, stained flooring, furniture destroyed. That sort of thing. The parents haven't been back to the house since the cops cleared it for them to return. They want everything repaired and cleaned up first. They were referred to us. Figured we could use the exposure."

"And money."

Always money. Dreams did not come true on wishes.

The Splatzes were known for their wild parties, loaded with the most delicious food. Or so she'd heard. This was the third party they had cleaned up after and still she felt the same as she had the prior times; a pang of disgust and a dash of dismay at all the leftovers. It was obscene that these people could waste so much when even in their small town, there were the less fortunate, people who would commit crimes to take even a sample of the food left behind. The waste was everywhere, spread over the Splatz's twelve-seater table, covering the large, oval island in the kitchen, discarded plates and glasses in all the common areas, trays of hardened finger foods set up throughout the multiple rooms downstairs. There always seemed to be enough left over to feed an additional twenty people. Maybe more, if no one gorged themselves.

The first time she and Allie cleaned up a party, they spent at least three-quarters of an hour moaning about the waste, bewildered at the laziness of leaving everything out to spoil. Delicate cheese puffs, savory tarts, some sort of whole fish with its head still attached, one baleful eye staring up at the ceiling, cakes, pies, horseradish whipped potatoes, eggs filled with something green and topped with mushrooms, grilled meats, smoked salmon, dips and crudites, fresh loaves of bread now hardened around the edges. All of it picked over and then left where it sat.

Now, on their third job cleaning up the gluttony, they didn't discuss the food or the mess. Nothing was surprising in the Splatzs' house. Not the plates under the sofa or the several empty champagne glasses tipped like bowling pins in the restroom. Not the crumbs trailed up every step to the second floor or why there was a spicy jalapeno dip smeared on the game room curtains. The aftermath of the parties seemed more like what a herd of unsupervised toddlers would leave behind than well-to-do adults. It boggled Dee's mind to the point where she had to not think about it if she wanted to do the job. Trying to get into the head of her clients and their guests would only slow her down.

Three hours later, they gathered their gear, exiting through the garage, when Allie stopped her again. They watched the old man wander back up the sidewalk, thin lipped smile, placid eyes, the whole thing all over again. He nodded to them, and they nodded back, holding themselves rigid until he'd passed beyond the next house, turned a corner, and finally moved out of sight.

"Why does he make me feel like a naughty child?"

Dee exhaled slowly. "Like he wants us to know he's watching, so we'd better not step out of line?"

Allie nodded. "Yes, exactly like that."

"I am a twenty-seven-year-old woman, and I will not be intimidated by some harmless old man." She stomped her foot to punctuate the point, but then realized the action probably looked ridiculous and absolutely not something a mature person would do.

"Sure thing, Dee," Allie snorted. "Keep telling yourself that."

She would keep telling herself that, repeating it in her head until she grew sick of her own voice. Someday, she would have to accept that she was responsible, that she had grown out of the people pleaser she had always been. She would stand up for herself. She would tell some-one, *No, sorry, I can't help you right now. I'm busy.* And she would mean it, even if she wasn't busy. Someday, she would demand a bakery clerk pay enough attention to her so she could order more than a strudel and not have to go from one job to another with a hole in her stomach. Which, considering all the food they'd just tossed, she should be too irritated to be hungry. But, no, that wasn't how hunger worked. And, honestly, she should have packed something. This was her own fault, not the counter clerk from Mrs. Leckermaul's. Besides, she poked at her thigh, she could skip a meal or two.

"Stop doing that," Allie barked, easing Bertha into gear.

"Doing what?" Dee blinked at her.

"Stop," Allie's hand waved in her direction, "judging yourself. You are perfect. Your hair is the most insane shade of red, you are curvy, kind, and the most over-the-top helpful person I know. I won't let you poke at that thigh and scowl. The thigh deserves better."

If there was one thing Allie did not lack, it was confidence. And why not? When people paid just for the honor of watching you on their screen, you could afford to be confident.

"Now, where the hell are we going? Let's get this kidnapping scrubbed away. I have things to do."

Chapter Three

YACHT CLUB CAT LITTER

The signs of struggle were everywhere in the client's house. She and Dee exchanged a knowing glance. They wouldn't earn what this job was worth, but they would do their best. Allison sometimes begrudged that Dorseigh was a better person than her, but today, she'd just do her job. This family deserved to feel safe.

All the fixable things were set to rights. They hauled whatever couldn't be repaired to the truck. All that was left now was cleanup.

As Allison schlepped the vacuum into the living space, a gleaming *something*, under the cushion of the cream sofa with an array of custom designed throw pillows, caught her eye. The object was so small, and they'd found so many bits of flotsam and jetsam, that Allie almost missed it and would have sacrificed the precious piece to the vacuum gods. However, the curious shiny item did not want that. No. Not at all. It screamed, *"See me!"*

With a press of a button, she switched the vacuum off, squatting to get a closer look. The object wasn't made of glass, but a silver—no *platinum*—rabbit charm with a diamond chip eye!

Damn shame that would have been if you went missing, pretty girl, she thought to herself.

Allie pinched the rabbit between her fingers and pocketed the charm. It felt warm and comforting there in her pocket. A smile curved her lips. She would put it on her bracelet when she got home. Then she could wear it all the time.

"What are you doing?"

Allie's heart lurched at the sound of Dee's voice. What *was* she doing? These people lost a kid, and she'd stolen jewelry. It could belong to the victim, maybe even the suspect. Her hand moved toward the pocket, but she didn't get it out. Her head swam, and her stomach threatened to revolt if she made any move to reveal what she had hidden.

"What was that?"

This couple had had something horrible happen to their children. She should show Dee the charm and tell her she was going to place it somewhere safe. She wanted to tell her friend, but her mouth seemed to have a mind of its own. "Hmmm? What was what?"

Plastering on a smile, she shook her own charm bracelet. "Dropped one."

Dee narrowed her eyes and chewed her bottom lip.

Allie's heart pounded as fast as if she were a real rabbit staring up the barrel of a hunter's gun.

Finally, her friend said, "Do that vacuum pattern on the cushions you do for the special clients. It'll be something nice for them to come home to." She sighed. "They've been through so much."

Guilt turned her stomach into leaden knots. She should fess up. Say she thought the charm was hers, but it wasn't.

No. No. Don't give up the charm. It now belongs to someone who won't be so careless with it. Maybe if they weren't always at social events, they wouldn't have had their children kidnapped. Besides it was only a small thing the vacuum would've swept up anyway. They'll never miss it.

Smile still frozen on her face, Allie nodded and started the vacuum again.

Later, Bertha glugged and sputtered and made a distinct whine as she drove from the client's house. The whole carriage shook. A far cry from the truck's condition this morning.

Allie couldn't help but feel like this was a retaliation from the universe for stealing from the family who'd lost kids.

Dorseigh let out a groan.

Their friend Leander would fix the truck for practically free, but they both didn't need the extra cost of the parts. He would try giving them the parts, too, but Dee had a Midwest, not-owing-anyone-anything attitude. Allison didn't understand it, but it was also an endearing trait of her business partner and friend. Dee cheated no one. Allie felt safe, even if she could no longer say the same.

As if to comfort her and say the opposite was true about her character, the charm warmed in her pocket. The warmth spread, washing out all the discomfort of guilt.

It wasn't like she had stolen from poor people. She was kinda like Robin Hood, really. Except, Allie was the poor to whom she gave the loot...

Another splutter and jerk from the truck. "The ol' girl's in trouble, Dee."

"Sounds like we're going to need Leander."

Allie looked at Dee, not surprised there was a grin on her friend's face that matched the smile in her tone. If her friend knew that the big oaf gave her the same sort of puppy dog eyes when she wasn't looking, she'd likely run for the hills. Dorseigh McHale had the worst case of insecurity which made zero sense to Allison. The woman had natural beauty in spades and was a genuinely kind person.

"How about we head home so you can take Kansas with you? He makes a better third wheel than I do." That would give her time to get the charm settled nicely on her bracelet. Also, the statement was a nice little payback for the morning's bakery clerk teasing.

Dee's cheeks colored crimson, and she gave Allie a wide-eyed innocent look. Her red lips made a perfect "O" of shock. "Why would you be a third wheel?"

Allison bit the corner of her lip to keep from laughing. "Come on. The guy is crazy about you."

"Lee is just a friend," Dee stammered, filling in the silence. "You're not a third wheel at all! He likes you, too. Well, not *like like,* as in attracted to you—" She paused and gulped some air.

Was Dee aware she was fanning herself?

"I mean, if he is attracted to you, he hasn't said, b-bu-but you know what I mean. Right?"

Allie wanted to say, *"the lady doth protest too much,"* but Dee might melt into the seat from any further ribbing. "Uh-huh. Right."

Dee crossed her arms and made the cutest pouty face. "You're teasing me because you want to game and not be stuck at the garage all evening."

"Glad you caught on." She winked, letting her friend off the hook before the woman's entire face and neck turned crimson.

Dorseigh laughed, and her stiff posture relaxed a little. Better for her to think Allie wanted to game than for both to stew in a broth of awkward denial. The secondhand embarrassment was too much.

Besides, Dee was sort of right. Allie would rather spend her evening setting the charm to its rightful place and then gaming and swiping through the millionaire dating app than go to the garage. The feet shuffling and bashful exchange of glances between Dee and Leander was too much for her to bear without intervention.

The truck's engine trouble grew louder.

"I hope the old girl will make it to Leander's shop."

Allison's gut knotted in agreement with Dee's statement. She'd just maxed out her credit card on shoes. She didn't want to rack up another bill. "Think he'll charge?"

The question caused the blush to spread from her friend's cheeks to her ears and neck. Biting her lip, Dee shook her head.

Allie wanted to tease her friend about ways she could pay him back, but she got no enjoyment out of embarrassing her friend.

Bertha was kind enough to get them home.

As soon as she put the old girl in park, she tossed Dee the keys. "Say hi to Lee for me!"

~

The castle guard put up a good fight. An excellent fight, actually. Allie almost got her player's head lopped off, but someone had her back. A sword tip pierced the armor of the knight she was fighting. Blood from the NPC, gushing in the wake of a player running through the guard with a blade.

Mr. Purrkins played a grizzled, retired mercenary that had enough add-ons and specialized weapons to signal that the Mr. Purrrkins had some extra cash in the real world.

Allie sighed.

He probably lived in some podunk east coast town, in his parents' basement, and spent all his money on this game. It was a silly stereotype, but she thought it was safer to imagine than to get involved with another gamer. This was her income. Her second job. She never mixed work and dating.

"Thanks," she said over the mic. "Spared me a life."

"Always willing to serve," Mr. Purrkins' voice purred from the speaker of her headphones. His player bowed with a flourish then went back into the fray.

A shiver of pleasure danced down her spine. He had a silly username, but his sexy voice did things to her, especially when he said things like that.

If only the game were real. If only she were a gentry turned street urchin after the queen killed her family and he an ex merc with some sort of sad backstory. How much more interesting than a handy person who streamed at night to feed her expensive tastes and a ... whatever he did for work that made him have to go to bed early.

They'd met on a server when she wanted to start this campaign. He was always polite, never flirted, or at least not like other guys. Definitely not in an overt way like the guy at the bakery. She rolled her eyes at the way he thought pastries were enough to seduce her.

The thing was, Allison also had no idea what Mr. Purrkins looked like. He wasn't a streamer, but he should be. He was her fans' favorite. Maybe he was too hideous to stream? That thought should make her pulse stop racing. Yet, it didn't. She liked the way he looked out for her and never teased her when she messed up and almost got her player killed. Chivalrous in the true sense of the word.

Speaking of her stream, the live chat was going wild over something. She scrolled through the comments.

You're blushing

Do you want to smash the merc?

Allie flipped off the camera. That got more reactions. Some gifts and money. *Ugh. Why do they love it when I'm mean to them?*

Her phone buzzed with a message notification. Normally, she ignored those on a livestream, but she caught a bit of the message on her screen. It was someone from a dating app that she was playing a long game of seduction with. Someone with a yacht club membership.

Somehow, she found her voice, announcing to her team and her viewers, "I have to go ... um... Family emergency." She was already logging out of the game.

"Oh, no! Hope everything is okay, Wandergirl," Mr. Purrkins's voice in her headphones held enough concern to cause her a twinge of guilt for the lie.

Ugh. Why did his feelings about this matter? He was just some stranger on the internet. Instead of replying, she logged out of everything else and shut her camera off.

Allie blew out her breath and opened the messenger on her dating app.

I had a business dinner canceled at the last minute, but my reservation for seven at the yacht club still stands. Can you meet me there? The view will make an excellent first date. My treat, of course.

x,

T

She closed her eyes and held her phone to her chest, squealing and kicking her feet. A niggling voice asked if she was excited to see him or go to the yacht club? She told it to shut up. She was going on a date with a man who owned his own business and traveled the world!

Rabbit scratched away at his litter box, and the foul stench that followed drew her out of her giddy head spin. Her gaze flicked to the calendar. It was litter box cleaning day. If she didn't do it, Rabbit would start grabbing items from her room and plopping them in his litter box while she was out.

She texted back: *I'll need a little wiggle room on the time, but I'd love to have dinner with you.*

She was surprised to see an immediate text back.

Making me wait? How saucy!

"Saucy?" She grimaced at the screen. "Who says *saucy*?" Allie decided not to reply to that. The response was a little quirky, but even rich people get nervous, right?

～

The clock on her phone read quarter past seven when Allie stepped out of the cab. Saltwater scented the air, and the murmur of conversation drifted from the outdoor patio of the restaurant adjacent to the yacht club located on a pier, central to the marina itself. Yachts of varying sizes lined the piers; some spaces were left open by those who'd ventured out for a dinner cruise around the harbor.

Upon entering the restaurant, a host greeted her with a smile. "Ms. Allison?"

She nodded rather than answering, feeling an old armor set into place at the mention of her given name. A few people looked in her direction, but no one recognized her. She'd changed so much since the last time she ate among the town's elite. Time and sinking into abject poverty will do that.

The host led her to a table where a man with salt and pepper hair was seated. Her heart sank a little. She didn't mind a little older, but he'd had brown hair in the pictures and his profile had said he was thirty-eight. That was twelve years older. Manageable. This man had to be at least about ten years older than his profile pics and ostensible age. Twenty-two years was too big of an age gap. What would they even talk about?

Another part of her worried he ran in the same circles as her mother. She hated that he'd made her think of that woman.

Her date rose to greet her, hand forward. She took it limply. Her stomach churned and gurgled. She'd walked away from a campaign for a man that was a big fat liar. *This catfish better be rich.*

"Sounds like someone's hungry!"

Allison smiled blandly. Food was the last thing on her mind. How to make an escape without her getting a bad rating on the app was front and center.

"I'm Theodore on the app, but you may call me Teddy."

Theodore the clothier. He owned a chain of posh boutiques of tailor-made clothing, supposedly around the world. He had said he didn't want to mention which boutique because of "privacy reasons." Now, she was doubtful that was true either. His clothes were well made, though. Meticulous. Even his hair didn't have a single flaw, besides the grey.

He smiled at her awkwardly. "Do you go by Allison or—"

"Allison works."

She felt his eyes on her body as she took her seat, and he pushed in her chair. She wore a tasteful, black cocktail dress that hinted at her figure and décolletage but wasn't too particularly low cut, and kitten heels. She was going for a subdued look for the first date that would coordinate perfectly with the outfits he wore in his profile pictures. It went with what he wore now, but she didn't want to match this dinosaur.

Teddy smiled as he took his seat and whispered behind his hand. "Everyone here seems to want a peek at you. Probably wondering how the geezer bagged the Instagram model."

Except, his whisper wasn't a whisper at all but a stage aside, whisper-shouted loud enough for everyone to hear.

Allie's cheeks heated. He'd called her an Instagram model—something anyone could profess—and she'd noted the distinction. He was saying she wasn't pretty enough for magazines and runways. How was she supposed to respond?

Thankfully a server approached.

"I got it," her date said, holding up a hand. Teddy ordered a bottle of Cristal champagne and a few hors d'oeuvres for the table.

Allie dug her nails into her palms. She wasn't a child and didn't appreciate being ordered for. "How thoughtful. I haven't even gotten a chance to look at the menu."

"I can't believe this client of mine," Teddy started in as if she hadn't said anything. "She wants all of my time, needing to see the next season's line before anyone else, as if I'm her personal shopper, not running a business. I must foot the bill at places like this, and she had the nerve to text me, 'I'm in a mood. My person will reschedule for next week....'" He droned on about the woman and her entitlement and how he had to basically let her emasculate him.

"Women just aren't like they used to be." His eyes darted to her chest. "Not like you. You are the pinnacle of classic femininity."

Like when you were young in the stone ages. She lifted her water glass and took a sip. Her hand shook with rage. Yacht Club money or not, she wanted nothing to do with this creep.

Before she could set the glass down and say the date was over, he snarled, "Where did you get that?"

His tone and expression had gone from an awkwardly misogynistic jerk to a feral kind of anger that made not only Allison, but the people around them jump.

Uncomfortable with his question and the number of people who gawked at the interaction, she answered in a low voice, "The glass was on the table."

His hand darted across the table, grabbing her wrist in a vice-like grip. "No, silly girl. The charm. Where did you get it?"

She yanked, but his grip was too solid for her to break free. Panic set in. Allie swallowed hard. Did he know the client she'd stolen from?

He knows nothing. He just wants what's yours. Dirty liar.

She steeled herself to deny anything he might claim at any cost. He wouldn't take what was hers. "Which one?"

He shook her arm, and the charms jingled with the movement. "The hat with the fancy band. Where did you get it?"

Amidst the sea of panic, a clear thought occurred, buoying her from drowning. There were six charms on her bracelet. None of which was a hat with a fancy band. If she denied it existed, this weirdo might get worse. "A gift from my late mother. Now let me go."

Teddy's eyes narrowed and his mouth set in a grim line, but he let go.

Skin ablaze from the tenacity of his grip, Allie rubbed her wrist and stood.

He shook his head, slumped in his seat, and then gave her an apologetic look. "I'm sorry. You probably think I'm very odd. The charm looked like something my late wife owned. I'd given it to her upon our second anniversary. It was an impossibility. Kathy—my late wife—was buried with it, you see." He smiled ruefully into the distance. "Perhaps guilt that I'm on the first date since she passed overcame me. I—I am usually the model of decorum. I hope you'll forgive my behavior and give this date a second chance?"

A widower explained some things, like starting over at his age and not knowing that harping over some client wasn't great conversation with a woman you don't know, but what you'd shared with a spouse. Allie felt pity for him. Perhaps the photos were of the last time he was happy. Maybe he didn't realize how long ago they were taken? Grief was a strange thing. She'd experienced enough of it to know. Besides, if she walked out, everyone would remember this incident. If she sat and at least ate, she could walk away with some dignity, right?

She forced a smile. "Let's try again."

Dinner didn't get any better. Teddy decided it was time to talk about his late wife Elizabeth's cancer. He kept repeating, "She was just too good for this world." His eyes strayed to Allie's charm more often than to her chest.

At the end of the date, he paid and walked her outside. He grabbed her once more. This time was for a kiss. She broke it off.

"I have to go home."

"I know you're a good girl, Allison, not like the others on the app. It's in the way you dress and carry yourself. I don't want a one-night stand. I want to take care of you and protect you from the kind of men who would sully you. Come to my house for a nightcap. It'll be as chaste as you'd like it to be."

Sully? Was this guy for real?

As much as she knew this lonely man would be so easy to play into taking her on as wife number two and convince him to move out of a town with such bad memories, Allie found herself repulsed by the idea of being married to this sad, volatile man. That arm grab would not be the last either. It was just a taste of what was to come.

"I have a shoot early in the morning," she lied.

He grinned as if he believed it, but it didn't reach his eyes. "Can I at least give you a ride home?"

"Oh, I'm fine. My roommate is on her way." She turned away, looking for the rideshare she'd ordered in the restroom before they left.

"Is she?"

"Yeah."

Like magic, the car pulled up, ending the conversation. It did have a glowing sign, but she got in without saying another word.

When she got home, the house was dark. Allie sincerely hoped there would be an overnight for Dee. She got ready for bed in a glum mood. Finally, under the covers, she almost drifted off imagining that Mr. Purrkin's player had shown up to run that jerk at dinner through with his sword. The smell of used litter overpowered everything.

"Ugh!"

Pissed off at her past self, Allie threw off the covers and picked up the bag next to the box. She stomped all the way through the house, the back door banging behind her. Her anger almost caused her to miss the dead body lying between the bins.

Chapter Four

SOUP BEANS AND PHONE CALLS

*D*ee stood in the doorway watching her friend charm an elderly customer. Dee knew it was Mrs. Bell due to the two-seater bicycle parked outside the shop and from the old-fashioned hat perched somehow, miraculously, atop her fluff of white hair. Mrs. Bell was never seen without her hat or her bike. More miraculous than how the hat stayed on her head - Glue? Pins? Rubber cement? - was that the little old lady could still handle the bike even after her husband passed away last year. Or was it two years ago?

She was lucky Bertha had made the trip home and then back out to Leander's shop. While she didn't know the exact contents of Allie's bank account, she knew her own and what they had in reserve for the business. It wasn't dire, not yet, but paying for a tow—even the prospect of it—made her stomach turn just a bit.

Leander threw a quick wink Dee's way before refocusing on Mrs. Bell and her issue—a dripping faucet, from what Dee could understand. She gritted her teeth at the blush that instantly rose on her cheeks. A blush. From a stupid, nothing wink.

At various points in her life, she'd tried to toughen up, either by changing a look or her makeup or by reading several self-help books. None of them worked beyond a surface level. She could hold her own and had done so for most of her life, but inside? Inside she was a mess of nerves and guilt.

Once she realized changing the outside would not change the inside, she'd donated all the new clothes. They hadn't protected the well of empathy that constantly bubbled inside her anyway. Plus, she didn't really relate to the music or the people. They were fine and all, some of them even softer than her, but it was a lot of work to play a person you weren't. These days, she wore jeans and tees and some-times, when she was especially crazy, flannel. She'd kept the boots, though. She liked the boots.

Mrs. Bell fluttered, her voice quivering with excitement when Leander promised he'd be over later to check out the faucet. When "later" would be was anyone's guess. Leander's internal clock did not follow any set pattern as far as Dee could tell. Besides, if she were a gambler, she'd bet Mrs. Bell broke that faucet herself, probably in a bathroom she rarely used. Chances were high she could wait to get it fixed.

When Mrs. Bell opined the seriousness of the leak, Dee decided to put her theory to the test.

"I could come and take a look right now, Mrs. Bell."

Mrs. Bell jumped, her thin hand clutched to her chest. "Oh, dear, I didn't know you were there." She squinted at Dee from behind glasses thick enough to make her eyes half their normal size. "What did you say, dear?"

Dee took a step further into Leander's small shop, keeping a hand on Kansas's head. He was off leash, which wasn't a normal habit. When she was out with him, he was leashed because she knew what people thought of big dogs. Especially Dobermans. Even with his floppy ears, people would shrink away, crossing the street or ducking into stores or yards, as if he were on the verge of turning feral. She didn't think there'd be anyone at Leander's this late in the afternoon, because usually there wasn't. She'd retrieved him from his crate and headed to the shop without a thought of grabbing his leash.

Truly, she didn't understand why Leander even had a shop. He was a handyman and a mechanic. He could work out of his garage if he wanted. But, no, instead he rented a small bay-front store that was nearly empty save for a counter for him to lean on, an empty register, and shelves holding various knick-knacks and baubles. The last time she was in his shop, she'd brought her duster to sweep over the worthless junk he insisted made the shop look respectable. She insisted it made the shop confusing and cluttered. In her head, of course. She would not tell him how to run his business.

"I said I would be happy to come and take a look at your faucet right now." She smiled brightly. She knew that smile brought to mind innocence and sweetness. She'd used it on her uncle whenever she'd been on the edge of not getting her way. Maybe it would work on Mrs. Bell, maybe it would win her over. "I have a bit of free time."

Mrs. Bell was not won over, though. "Oh, no, dear. I couldn't ask you to do that. Leander is my handyman. He has been for years. It wouldn't be right to take my business elsewhere."

Dee barely held in a snort. If Mrs. Bell had ever paid one single cent for any of the work done in her house, Dee would find a hat and eat it. There was not one possible point in time when Leander made money from fixing the old lady's leaky faucets. Also, she knew for a fact Mrs. Bell had not called Leander to fix things when her husband was still alive. Years her butt.

"It's okay, Mrs. Bell. I wouldn't mind if you needed immediate assistance." Leander somehow said the words with an entirely straight face, never mind the twinkle in his eye.

"No, no. I'll wait. I'll fix a late dinner for us, then?" She patted Leander's forearm where it rested on the countertop. "Around seven?"

"Sure thing, Mrs. Bell."

They both watched her leave the shop, skirting around where Kansas sat with his tongue dangling, his whip-like tail moving a hundred miles an hour, paws tapping on the floor as he impatiently waited for a head pat that wouldn't be coming from Mrs. Bell. She moved well for a frail old lady, deftly mounting the unwieldy bike and peddling away.

"Someone should get her a scooter," Dee mused, stepping further into the shop. "She's going to break a hip one day."

Leander straightened, scratching the red scruff on his face. "Nah.

She's a tough old bird." He stepped around the counter and knelt. "Come on, then," he said, a room-brightening smile splitting his face.

Kansas launched himself into Leander's waiting arms.

If there was anything more pathetic than being jealous of your dog, Dee didn't know what it was. She didn't even want to know what it was, because it would probably resemble her.

She kicked the toe of one boot against the concrete block Leander used to prop the door open on hot days, the blush rising before she worked up the courage to speak, to bring up the reason she was there. "Bertha might be dying."

Both eyebrows, the same color as his scruff, shot up. He was a mismatched conglomeration of features, things that should fight against each other instead of somehow working together. He shouldn't be as handsome as he was. "Sounds serious." Dirty blond hair, the dark red scruff and eyebrows, dark eyelashes, light brown eyes. Tallish and thick, so damn thick. "Dee?"

She blinked. She'd been staring, transfixed on his thighs like the blushing virgin she imagined everyone thought her to be. "What?"

"Bertha." He patted Kansas and stood. "You need me to take a look?"

Her phone buzzed from her back pocket, shaking her all the way back to the present, back from ogling a man who had never shown any interest in her beyond friendship. She should be a little ashamed of herself, truth be told. How old did a person need to be before they left schoolgirl crushes behind?

Swallowing a sigh, she pulled out the phone and then the sigh escaped anyway. "It's Aunt Sal. But, yeah, Bertha's making some pretty unfortunate noises."

"Then I'll take a look while you take that call." He twisted his hair into a low, messy knot that somehow looked good on him, but would make her look like she skipped a few showers. "C'mon boy. Let's give your mom some privacy."

Like a dog loyal to more than one master, Kansas followed him outside.

"Traitor," Dee muttered before answering the call. "Hey, Aunt Sal."

"Dee! I'm surprised you answered the phone. I thought maybe you didn't want to talk to me anymore."

Dee counted back to how many days it had been since she'd spoken to her aunt and uncle. They'd discussed the missing kids. Was it five kids now? Six at the most. Regardless, it was maybe four days. Four at the most. Which, yes, could be considered a long time, but not unreasonable. If Aunt Sal had her way, they'd be on the phone at least once a day, just to talk about the weather. Too bad Dee hated talking on the phone. Having to take and schedule jobs was bad enough. She did not have it in her to carry on mindless conversations with her aunt. Or anyone. And that was why she'd never get anywhere with Leander. Leander was full of mindless conversations. Well, that and he was objectively too attractive to ever notice her.

Stars and stripes, she needed her brain to stop dragging him into every conversation she had with herself. It was annoying. And pointless. And a little depressing, to be perfectly honest.

"I'm sorry, Aunt Sal. There's been a lot on my plate this week." A lie. Sort of. Other than the day's earlier jobs, the last week had been sort of slow. Her aunt didn't know that, though.

"I've called three times, sweetheart, did you see that?"

Of course she had. "Well, yes, but—"

"Well, you should have answered. We've been worried about you out there with that maniac snatching up those kids. We need to know you're safe. Two more were taken just this week. Did you hear?"

Obviously, since she and Allie had just spent the bulk of the afternoon cleaning up the aftermath.

An image flashed through her mind. Allie picking something off the floor. She'd said it was a charm from her bracelet, but Dee didn't remember seeing a missing charm when Allie shook the bracelet at her. Of course, Dee didn't spend much time thinking about Allie's charm bracelet, mostly because Allie didn't generally wear jewelry to jobs.

"Dorseigh Marie, are you listening to me?"

The memory vanished, snapping her back to the present. "Yes, of course I'm listening. I'm just," she sighed. "We're having trouble with the truck. I'm at the mechanic's. I'm sorry. It's just been a long day."

Her aunt's voice softened as she said, "You poor thing. You're overworked. Why don't you come over later and I'll make us a nice dinner. Your uncle would love to see you, you know."

Sure, why not. Maybe Leander would drop her off on his way to "fix" Mrs. Bell's leaky faucet. Otherwise, she'd have to walk to the outskirts of town with an unleashed dog. With her luck, she'd for sure get a citation.

"That sounds great, Aunt Sal. I'll be over soon."

"Whenever you can get here will be fine. I've had soup beans on all day. I just need to make the cornbread."

Soup beans. It would have to be soup beans. How many meals did she spend as a kid finding ways to get rid of soup beans without eating them? If Aunt Sal made them with ham or literally anything other than bland navy beans, maybe she would like a big bowl of soup beans. But, no, flavor was outside Aunt Sal's purview. She didn't even know why they ate the stuff, other than the cost. She hadn't met anyone else who'd ever been subjected to eating it. Other than her Uncle Hank, considering they were his favorite.

"Okay, great, keep them warm for me."

Her aunt and uncle didn't drive much anymore, but they would find a way to get her if she couldn't make it to them. Especially now that she'd agreed to dinner. A natural disaster would be about the only thing to prevent her from suffering through a bowl of beans.

One could dream.

On the street, Leander was under Bertha's hood, the sleeves of his brown flannel rolled to his elbows, showing off the world's best forearms.

No, she scolded herself. *Focus. Focus on your truck. Focus on how much this will cost, how inconvenient it will be to go without your truck while it is being repaired. Do not look at his forearms. You are not an old maid who has never seen a man's bare arms before.*

Kansas lay patiently on the curb, ears perked, staring up at the man like it was he who hung the sun. She plopped down beside him, throwing an arm over his back. He looked at her long enough to lick her chin, his tail giving a thump, thump before he resumed his worshipful gaze.

"What's the damage?" Dee asked, purposefully staring at the under-side of the hood and not at the large man two feet in front of her.

He stopped messing around in the guts of the truck long enough to give Dee a quick glance. "Nothing too major, shortcake. Carburetor, probably. Might need a new air filter." He rolled his shoulders before slamming the hood. "I can probably have it back to you in a day or so."

She winced. Not ideal, but there weren't exactly a lot of options.

"You okay?" To her shock, he lowered himself beside her, Kansas practically crawling over her lap to get closer to him. He nudged her arm with his elbow. "You look like you're facing a firing squad."

She gave him a small smile. "Worse. My aunt's cooking."

"Aw. Poor Dee." He laughed, his big hand on Kansas's head. "Can't be that bad, can it?"

"It is," she said in a sober, solemn tone. "You have no idea. You'll be having some wonderfully home cooked meal with Mrs. Bell and I'll... Well, I'll also have a home cooked meal, but it will not be wonderful."

At this, his laugh turned into a guffaw. "Have you ever been in Mrs. Bell's house? Cats, Dee. So many cats. All of them hissing and spitting at me. The whole place smells of piss and do not ask me about the hair. Trust me, you will have a better time."

"Hissing and spitting?" Dee was suddenly very thankful for Rabbit, who never hissed or spat. And, of course, thankful to Allie for never letting the house smell like cat pee. "You should have let me go to her house. Then we'd both be safe from horrible dinner plans."

"My hero." He fluttered dark lashes, throwing an arm over her shoulders. "Next time, Dee. Next time, she is all yours."

~

*D*ee wouldn't say that dinner was good. She would *never* say that about bland beans, but it wasn't as bad as her memories conjured. At least she enjoyed the time with her aunt and uncle. Consid-ering they were her only family left. They'd been old when they took her in at twelve without a moment's hesitation and had never complained about any of her activities in high school—at least not where she could hear—she really should make more of an effort to help them. Too bad life kept getting in the way. It was nearly twenty minutes to get to their house from hers and sometimes after a day of deep cleaning the floor in a downtown office after a pipe burst or replacing gutters on the mother's house on the west side of town, the one with all the kids and no husband to help around the house, she was bone tired. Sometimes it was all she could do to wash her own dishes after making a lame dinner. Still, watching her aunt, nearly as frail as Mrs. Bell, flutter around her tiny kitchen and Uncle Hank slowly make his way from the beat-up recliner in the front room to the wobbly table in the dining room, she resolved to make the time. These were the people who raised her, who had taken her in when she had no place else to go. The memories of her parents were faint, ever fading, sometimes impossible to pull up. But her aunt and uncle were right here, still within reach, and she should make sure they knew how much she appreciated what they'd done for her.

After dinner, she had planned on cleaning up, on pulling out the ancient dishwasher Aunt Sal complained had stopped working. She'd planned on putting her resolve into action.

But then her phone started buzzing, Allie's name flashing across the screen. She considered ignoring it, but Allie never called, always texted. She might be hurt or worse. She held up a finger to Aunt Sal, to pause in telling her aunt that she would get the dishwasher fixed, and answered the phone.

"There's a boy," Allie screamed. "A boy! He's in our yard, Dee! I think he's dead. Where did he come from? I don't know what to do!"

Between one escalating beat of Dee's heart and the next, she thought maybe she should stop answering the phone.

"Call the police, Allie," she said to her roommate, holding up a hand at her aunt's alarmed look. "I'll be there as soon as I can."

"Don't hang up," Allie cried. "What if he's dead?"

"Then you should call the police. I will be right there." She muted her phone. "I need your car, Aunt Sal. I swear I'll bring it back tomorrow."

Which is how she ended up driving a twenty-year-old Prius across town, pushing it to a top running speed of forty miles per hour as promised to her aunt and uncle, headed towards whatever catastrophe that had been tossed into her backyard.

In mere minutes, she beat the police to her house. Which meant Allie had probably stood frozen in the backyard for who knew how long before she managed to make the 9-1-1 call. She'd just managed to secure Kansas in her room and make it to the back door when the street out front flooded with flashing lights.

"Allie," she called, stepping into the yard.

Her best friend, her roommate, and her business partner stood paralyzed, arms wrapped around her chest, tears streaming down her perfect face. "There," she whispered. "In there."

The police pounded on the front door, demanding to be let in. Before she moved, before she saved their door from being smashed in, she shone the flashlight on her phone to the trash bins, to where Allie's horrified gaze was riveted, to see a boy, maybe eleven or twelve, fully dressed thankfully, but so pale he was nearly gray and so still she didn't know how he could be anything but dead.

"I'm going to get the door, Allie." She pocketed her phone and held her roommate by the shoulders. "It's going to be okay." She led her back inside, through a mudroom and to the small kitchen table before sprinting to the front door, shushing Kansas on the way.

She threw open the door to...

"What are you doing here?"

The baker's assistant stood on her steps, dressed in jeans and a snug black henley.

He stared at her blankly, as if he'd never seen her before. Of course.

"There was a call about a body," he said calmly.

"Yeah, but—"

"It's okay. I'm a fireman," he informed her abruptly.

Fireman? "We called the police?"

"Out of the way, Sourire." A stocky cop with ash blond hair and a deeply unpleasant face pushed the baker's assistant aside. "Where's the body, ma'am?"

Dee couldn't be certain, since she didn't know how the name was spelled, but she was almost positive the cop did not pronounce the baker's assistant's name in any way correctly.

She led the two men, followed by three more uniformed police and one plain-clothed woman, through the house to the backyard. She didn't fail to notice how the baker's assistant—*Sourire*—nearly tripped over himself when they passed through the kitchen, where Allie blankly watched the procession. Once outside, she led the police to the body before being hustled back inside.

"Is he dead?" Allie asked in a small voice, which did something to the bottomless maternal instinct that was the heart of Dee's being.

"I don't know." She grabbed Allie's cold hand, holding it in both of hers.

The answer came a quarter of an hour later when an ambulance screamed up the street, Sourire jogging through the house to lead the paramedics to the yard. He stepped back into the kitchen a few seconds later.

"He's not dead," he informed them solemnly. Or, Dee suspected, as solemnly as he could be. His face was placid, but something danced in his eyes, his lips twitching ever so slightly at the corners.

Allie sobbed in relief.

Paramedics took the boy, followed by a few, unpleasant minutes of questions from the hard-faced cop—Detective Doyle—who didn't treat them like suspects, but also not like innocents.

"Don't leave town," he told them as they both followed him to the front door. "We might have more questions for you."

Chapter Five

MIRACLES AND ALLEGATIONS

S piky mallets hammered at the back of Allison's eyes. She swallowed back two ibuprofen and washed it down with water over the sink. Worry, something she was unused to, formed tiny, barbed knots in her gut.

Finished crating an over-excited Kansas, Dee entered the kitchen. As usual, her skin looked enviably fresh and dewy without makeup, except for the unusual-for-Dee dark smudges that had formed under her eyes.

Apparently, neither of them had gotten much sleep. How could they? A boy, barely a teenager, had lain seemingly lifeless between their recycling and refuse bins as if he were detritus blown in from the street, not a person on the cusp of adulthood. The thought rattled her more than she cared to admit.

Allison had seen plenty of dead bodies in video games, especially the one she played now. However, a three-dimensional rendering, gory or not, was nothing compared to finding a person in the state that kid had been. A memory tried to bubble its way up, but she pushed it down. *No. Video game violence was the worst I've seen.*

Eyes on the medication, Dee made grabby hands. Allie handed her the bottle of ibuprofen and a clean glass of water. Her roommate grunted her thanks and popped a couple pills in her mouth, gulping down the water like she was dying of thirst.

"Coffee from Black Forest Bakery?"

A glimmer of the usual Dee flashed in her eyes. "Mmm ... sounds good." Her shoulders then slumped, and she heaved a sigh. "I'm exhausted already."

Allie almost suggested that they took the day off, but she couldn't imagine sitting at home. Besides, they needed the money. She didn't feel like gaming either. Looking like crap wouldn't bring in any money. Maybe some pity coins, but that wasn't her brand. Besides, Dee wouldn't be able to make up for the cash lost missing a day of work, and they had however much money her friend would insist that they'd give Leander for the truck to consider.

Dee rinsed out the glass and placed it in the drying rack. "Last night was ... rough. You can stay home if you need to, but I got to go in."

"No way am I letting you pull three jobs by yourself." Allie wrapped her arms around her friend. Midwestern to the core, Dee stiffened at first and then accepted the hug, squeezing back.

"The kid will be okay."

Neither of them knew if that was actually true.

"Kids are resilient." Allie pulled back, examining her friend's face. "Sure is nice of your aunt to lend us the windup car until the truck is done."

Dee gave her a thin smile. Guilt flooded those pretty eyes of hers. "I didn't give her much choice."

In mutual miserable silence, they loaded the Prius with their gear. With the trunk and the rear packed tight with what they'd need, Allison drove them to their usual breakfast haunt.

By the time they entered Black Forest Bakery, her headache was gone, but not her worry for the kid. Her heart sank a little when she saw Mrs. Leckermaul was behind the counter instead of the clerk named Sourire. Allie wanted to catch up with the baker moonlighting as a volunteer firefighter to hear how the kid was doing.

"Gutentag!" Leckermaul's voice rang with unusual warmth, her smile too bright, too young for her erstwhile weathered face. Her normally dull eyes gleamed. Even the woman's skin seemed to glow. Maybe it was just her mood, but as she moved, she seemed more agile than before.

Allie exchanged glances with Dee. Judging from her friend's half-hearted shrug, she didn't have the energy to guess what was up with Mrs. Leckermaul either. They greeted the baker with muttered replies.

The shimmering attitude dimmed a little. The old woman eyed them through narrowed slits, as if suspicious of their lack of cheer. "Why so glum on such a lovely morning?"

The cop had said not to tell anyone anything about the investigation. Didn't he? At least that was the procedure in movies. Better safe than legally sorry.

"My date was a flop," Allie admitted, since it was *a* truth. Other demons lay in the shadows of the whole truth. Seeing that body sprawled out reminded her of another day. A day she swore to forget. Getting out of this town of constant reminders would help her. With the appearance of the kid and her flop date, that seemed like an impossible future for her.

A shadow flitted across the elderly woman's face, there and gone so fast Allison believed she imagined it. She grinned. "Is that all? You look as if someone died."

The image of the boy, barely a teenager, discarded between their bins like trash, came unbidden. She blinked the image away, breathing deeply to ground herself in the moment.

Dee cleared her throat, thankfully, taking the baker's gaze off Allison. "Not someone, but our truck up and died yesterday. It's gonna cost us."

Leckermaul made a sound of disapproval that sounded like her usual cantankerous self and dismissed their woes with a wave of her hand. "A new man and a new truck will fix your problems. Both are easily gotten with youth and looks like yours." Normally, the baker wouldn't even ask about their lives, now she was handing out advice. "How about something sweet in the meantime?"

The baker loaded a few extra pastries and a loaf of bread, grinning. "To help you two sad sacks cheer up."

The food did cheer Allie up a bit. However, the magic of delicious pastries only lasted for so long.

At their first job site, Allie went through the motions of her tasks, but her mind wandered. As they worked, Dee didn't say much other than what was necessary. Normally, they bantered and gossiped about the people they worked for. Idle chit chat didn't seem right.

They sat under a tree in a park for lunch. The sky did its best to remember the sunny part of sunny California, instead of doing the Pacific Northwest thing and raining October through April.

Dee paused between bites of her croissant. "Did Mrs. Leckermaul seem ... off to you?"

"She did. She seemed...she seemed—" Allie had a hard time putting a finger on exactly what it was. "Unusually, chipper, but also..."

"It wasn't just her personality," Dee interjected. "Leckermaul has got to be my aunt's age, but she looked about ten years younger today."

"Maybe she got a little filler or Botox or maybe a facelift?"

"Wouldn't she have bruises? We see her almost every day except yesterday."

"Chemical peel?" She frowned and then answered her own question. "No. She didn't have time to heal."

Allie bit into her brötchen and moaned with pleasure. The baked goods had always given her the best foodgasms ever, but this was the best brötchen she'd ever eaten from Black Forest Bakery. "Maybe she's a witch?"

Dee examined her croissant and opened her mouth as if she wanted to say something but closed it again.

Allison had an idea. "Maybe Leckermaul got a new man and now the cobwebs are knocked off her nethers?"

Dee stared off, thoughtful. "Let's say she got work done and a new man. That doesn't explain something that bothered me. Usually, Mrs. Leckermaul moves with the same slowness that comes with age. She seemed—I don't know—more agile than someone her age should be."

"Yeah. Didn't Sourire mention yesterday something about her doing deliveries? Could your aunt handle that?"

"Not at all." A wry grin spread on Dee's lips. "You remembered his name."

Allison cut her friend a sharp look. "Stay focused. We're talking about Leckermaul looking and acting out of character."

Dee smirked but dropped the teasing. "Don't serial killers go through some sort of rush after they kill?"

Allison turned to fully face her. "That's a stretch. Mrs. Leckermaul is a grumpy baker, who either got some work done or got herself a new beau. If I were a cop, she wouldn't be on my list of suspects. Besides, there's nothing connecting Leckermaul to the missing kids."

With a pointed look, Dee said, "She runs a bakery."

Allie's stomach dipped.

The boy she'd found out back had just turned thirteen recently. She'd noticed candles and deflated balloons when she'd cleaned his parents' house. Could the baker be drugging birthday cakes, breaking in and taking kids in their sleep? She immediately dismissed that notion. "Leckermaul might be sprier and look younger, but he's a big kid. There's no way she hauled him to our backyard."

"Maybe he escaped her and hid there?"

"That's speculation. We need hard evidence if we want to bring it to the police's attention."

An alarm went off on her phone, indicating both lunch and the conversation were over.

~

The last job of the day left little room for more deliberation. An elderly couple were moving out of their house of fifty years into a small apartment in a retirement community. With the reduction of space from a four thousand square foot house with guest rooms to the one-bedroom place, most of the furniture had to go into storage.

Thankfully, they'd rented a container with a service that would haul it to the storage facility.

The elderly woman insisted on shambling next to Allie as the younger woman worked. She had silver hair wrapped in curlers under a scarf. She wore an old-fashioned housecoat with modern Crocs. Cats and balls of yarn adorned the holes in the shoes.

"My grandson would do this. He's very strong, but he's got a very important job here in town," the wife explained. Allison dreaded this sort of client. They looked over your shoulder every minute, just waiting to point out how she did something or the other wrong.

Dee mouthed, *"They're lonely."*

She always saw the best in people, which made her assumption about Mrs. Leckermaul so troubling.

From the front porch, the husband grunted, "He's a scrawny accountant who prefers his video games over worthwhile pursuits."

"Ha! Wonder where he gets it from. Don't you play chess at the park?"

The old man waved an age spot covered hand in dismissal. "Bah. That's not the same. It isn't natural to sit in front of a desk all day only to go home to another desk."

"My grandson drives a BMW from that desk to another desk in his home office! Bought his house outright. He'd make an excellent husband. You'd always know where he is, not like some of these roving dogs."

"Does he own his own firm or does he work for one?" Normally, Allie only feigned interest when some elderly client wanted to pawn off a single son or grandson, but if he was a home-owning, BMW-driving gamer, he probably racked up enough money to get out of here. At least thinking about it would get her mind off the boy.

Part of her felt a twinge of guilt for scheming while a kid was in the hospital, possibly dying. The other part was sick of working these jobs and humoring the clients while she did all their manual labor.

"It's his own firm," the lady confirmed proudly. "He has people working for him, but he likes to put in the same hours they do."

"Admirable."

Their grandson was sounding better and better. She was a gamer, too. Maybe they could bond over that? At least he wouldn't have a dead wife he wouldn't shut up about. She'd received no less than six texts from Teddy. Most were memes about forgiveness and love languages. *Barf.*

She pushed a dolly loaded with boxes out the door and down the ramp. The elderly lady followed her outside. Again. Suddenly, the chatter distorted, as if she spoke from a distance. Allie's knees buckled.

On the other side of the truck, a cop was putting handcuffs on Dee.

Another came from seemingly out of nowhere. An iron grip clamped Allie's arm. The couple talked in a frantic tone, but their words made no sense. The cop was saying something that sounded like a speech learned by rote, but she didn't understand him. Her vision tunneled on Dee's face.

She'd stolen the charm, but her friend hadn't ever done anything wrong in her entire life.

～

The interrogation room closed around her like a trap—stark walls, mirrored glass, two chairs and a table that had seen countless confessions. This wasn't some petty theft charge. They thought she was capable of something much worse.

Detective Doyle sat across from her, a study in calculated anachronism. Everything about him—from his old-fashioned collar to his pomade-slicked mustache—seemed designed to disarm. But his eyes behind those wire-rimmed spectacles were razor sharp, missing nothing.

Steam curled from his teacup as he watched her, letting the silence stretch. Memories she'd buried years ago clawed at the edges of her mind. Her pulse thundered in her ears.

"Your streaming alibis will take time to verify," Doyle finally said, his pen hovering over his leather-bound notebook. "But Mr. Chapeau can confirm your whereabouts last night?"

"Yes." The word caught in her throat. Teddy's unhinged behavior flashed through her mind. "Though the restaurant staff could—"

"Four children in comas, Miss Liddle." His voice cut like steel beneath the genteel accent. "Four families wondering if their kids will ever wake up. And you want to talk about restaurant staff?"

Ice slid down her spine. She knew exactly how those parents felt— what fear and rage could drive people to do. The memory rose like bile in her throat.

"You clean their houses, don't you?" Doyle continued, leaning forward. "Get close to the families. Learn their schedules. Build trust."

"That's not—"

"Tell me, what makes a young woman with your ... history ... choose to work in other people's homes? To get so close to their children?"

The bottom dropped out of her stomach. *He knows.* Maybe not everything, but enough.

"I didn't hurt those kids." Her voice came out stronger than she felt. "Run your checks. Talk to Theodore. I'm not what you think I am."

"No?" Doyle stood, his shadow falling across her. "Then tell me, Miss Liddle—what exactly are you?"

"Someone who learned her lesson a long time ago." She met his gaze steadily. "Check the yacht club."

He gathered his notebook. "For your sake, I hope your alibis hold. The parents in this town aren't as patient as I am. And they're very, very angry."

The threat hung in the air as he left her alone with her reflection—and the ghosts she thought she'd outrun.

***

Theodore admitted to the date, and Dee's aunt and uncle corroborated that she'd been at their place. However, the detective still thought that they'd had something to do with it.

Around three a.m., they made bail. Dee had talked about having her uncle take a loan out against the business to get them out. However, Leander had posted bail for them before she could ask. Or, at least they assumed he had signed for both of them. To both Dee and Allison's surprise, Sourire waited at the front desk next to Lee.

Dorseigh and Leander walked ahead of them, heads bowed in conversation.

"You're my responsibility. So, no skipping town. I believe you're innocent, but I won't lose my bond because you're scared and run," Sourire said as they walked out of the station.

Confused, Allie could only stare at the bakery clerk and volunteer firefighter. "Why would you do this for me? You don't know me, Sourire."

"Sourire is my last name. Call me Reuben." He grinned and leaned in, his voice a velvety purr, "What a cruel thing to say. We've done so many campaigns together. I'd like to think we're friends, if not close friends."

That velvet voice - the one that had guided her through countless virtual battles, made her pulse race through countless late nights - impossible, but undeniable. There was only one person who had a voice that could do that for her. It couldn't be. It was the only explanation for why he'd been so forward at the bakery and why he would do this for her.

"Mr. Purrkins?"

"Shhhh... Not here." He made a show of looking to the right and left, but Dee and Leander were the only ones around, and they were in their own world. He drew even closer. His breath was hot on her ear as he whispered, "I always have your back, Wandergirl."

Chapter Six

THE NOSE KNOWS

*B*eing bailed out by a man who, at best, viewed you as a cute kid sister, wasn't how Dee would have preferred to end any part of her day. Of course, being in jail wasn't something Dee could have envisioned. Nor being accused of hurting children. She didn't hurt anything if she could help it. She took spiders outside and opened windows for bees. She once nearly wrecked her aunt's car to avoid smooshing a squirrel as it darted across a road. She would *never* hurt a kid. And, yet, no matter how many times she'd reiterated that to the police, they didn't seem to care.

"You know," Leander mused, unlocking his rusty F-250, "I expect this sort of call from a lot of my friends, but I gotta say this surprised me."

Dee stared at the toes of her scuffed and slightly fraying work boots, barely visible in the yellow light from the dingy globe in Leander's truck. She didn't even know why he was there. She'd called her aunt and uncle. She would never have called Leander. He was going to talk about this day for ages. For as long as they remained friends. He would probably laugh about it with the next person he dated or the guy he drank with or even old lady Bell as he fixed some other conveniently broken appliance in her house. This is what he would attach to her, what he would remember her by. She would now always be the girl he had to bail out of jail, accused of harming children. He'd...

"Dee." One callused finger touched her chin, tilting her face upwards to look into his shadowed face. "Hey, don't worry. This kind of stuff always works itself out."

Yes, great. Awesome. Now she felt much better. Empty platitudes were what she needed at that moment.

Stuff like this worked out fine for people with money and lawyers. It did not work out for people like her. For Allie. Women who worked for themselves, making just enough to afford the basics. Women who, while not entirely on the outskirts of society, weren't exactly community darlings. Some people knew them, and they were liked well enough by those people, but they weren't anything special. At least, Dee wasn't. Allison had her streaming community and from all Dee knew about that, she *was* something special.

But here? In the real world?

"Are we going or what?" Allie asked from the passenger seat of the truck, her bakery-slash-volunteer-firefighter-slash-bail-payer-slash-whatever guy standing beside the open passenger door. Allie, in her true resilient fashion, only looked annoyed at the release, as if it had been a minor inconvenience for them. She'd felt okay enough to complain to Leander about the heaping piles of tools and flannels and discarded food wrappers that occupied the small back seat, forcing her into her current position.

"Up you go, shortcake."

Throat tight, eyes burning, Dee shook her head. "I think I'll walk." She took a backward step. "I need to—"

"Hey, no." Leander caught her by the arm before she could move further away. "It's the middle of the night. You aren't walking anywhere."

"I just," she jerked at her arm, but his hold remained tight. "I just need to, um," she swallowed down the knot of tension, of panic, of the need to burst into ugly, hideous sobs.

"C'mon, Dee." He tugged her forward a step, her nose pressing into his sternum. If he hugged her, she really would cry.

"It's fine." She pushed away right as he tried to wrap an arm around her back. "I'm fine. I won't walk. Let's go."

Feeling her eyes on his face, she resolutely refused to return the look. She couldn't. She could barely force the few steps to the truck, to jump onto the bench seat, to slide in beside Allie, who was also looking at her, concern etched into her equally tired face.

"I'm fine," she mumbled, staring at her hands now, shoved between her thighs.

Allie leaned close, her mouth pressing against Dee's ear. "Liar," she murmured. "We're innocent, Dee. We'll *prove* we are innocent."

But what about *until* they proved they were innocent? What happened when their clients all started to believe they had something to do with the harm of innocent children? They'd lose their business, their home. They'd have to move away from their friends and family. Well, Dee's family. She had no idea if Allie still spoke to her family. That was something they hadn't discussed since school. Allie's family wasn't a topic she brought up anymore, and Dee knew better than to push.

"Ready?" Leander asked, nudging her knee with his, either on purpose or because he could barely fit on the seat with Allie and Dee taking up so much room.

"God, yes." Allie said something to the bakery guy before powering up her window. "Please, let's get out of here."

Dee was aware, even in the darkened cab, that both Leander and Allie snuck glances at her. Even with a headache blossoming behind her eyes and the continued tightness in her throat, she wasn't unaware of their concern. Which was fine. They could be concerned, even though she wasn't fragile. Sure, she worried about things, but so did lots of people. Mothers. Mothers worried all the time, and no one snuck worried glances at them. She didn't mind their concern, but she didn't need it either.

She'd survived stuff before, she just needed sleep and to figure out their next steps.

The truck rolled to a stop and then was silent.

"Thank god." Allie was out the door and up the front porch steps before Dee even realized they were home.

"Come on. Let's get you in."

She heard Kansas's frantic barks as soon as Allie unlocked the front door, jolting Dee into movement.

"Oh, no! I haven't been home in hours. He's probably..."

"I took care of him, Dee. As soon as I heard, I fed them both and took him out. He's fine."

It was that act, his kindness towards her dog, that finally unraveled the tightness in her chest. A loud, unexpected sob escaped, followed by the flood of tears she'd hoped to keep locked in until she was alone in her room.

"Hey, here." Leander twisted her until her nose was pressed against his chest again, but this time his arms had her wrapped up before she could protest. Not that she would. All the fight, everything that had kept her upright the last few miserable hours was draining with her tears. "We're going inside," he announced, before dragging her out of the cab and walking her up the sidewalk, Kansas running out to bounce and whip his tail around, his joy at her return home enough to slow the tears.

"Hey, buddy." She knelt, accepting his kisses before Leander pulled her into the house, shutting and locking the door behind them.

"What are you doing?" She stood in the middle of the living room, wringing her hands. It was nearly four in the morning. They had a job to get to in a few hours and their lives to get in order. She couldn't entertain him right then, couldn't even imagine offering him a glass of water.

"Where's your room? I'm going to get you to bed and then I'm going to sleep on that uncomfortable looking couch in that room right there," he pointed towards the family room, "and if anything happens, I'll take care of it." Kansas chuffed an agreement.

"You don't have to do that."

"Dee, someone dropped a half-dead kid in your backyard. I'm staying. If I hear anything, I'm letting Kansas outside to scare the shit out of anything in your yard. I'm a little surprised he didn't scare off whoever was out there the other night. I bet he was going crazy."

"Maybe he did." She caressed her dog's floppy ears. "Maybe that's why they just tossed that little boy in the yard. Maybe they were planning on," she swallowed, "putting him in the house or something?"

"Then all the more reason I should sleep on your couch. You're one of my best friends. I'm staying." He crossed his arms over his chest, looking to her fuzzy brain like a ferocious leonine god. She blinked, and he was back to a guy with messy hair and a worn flannel. "Go to bed. To sleep. I'll take care of whatever happens between now and morning."

"It already is the morning," she mumbled, turning toward the stairs. She stopped once her hand landed on the banister, one foot on the bottom step. "Thank you. So much."

He said something, but her head was too full of cotton to hear. He'd already said more this evening than in any of the times they'd spent together. A *best friend*. How was she supposed to sleep with those words spinning around in her brain? No, forget that. How was she supposed to sleep when the actual police department thought she was a suspect in a kidnapping? And whatever else they thought. What was it they thought anyway? She'd have to remember to ask Allie in the morning.

Which came way too soon. She wasn't always the earliest riser. Sometimes Allie would still be awake from the night before, still streaming, still making money. But, usually, she was awake before the early parts of the morning had passed. Except, of course, for the mornings after she'd been arrested and spent half the night in a police station. That morning, she may never have woken up, if not for Kansas licking her face and somewhere further off in the house, Rabbit wailed like he was starving to death.

She cursed, gently pushing Kansas by the snout and sat up with a groan. Head pounding, eyes filled with sand, she reached for her phone and cursed again. They needed to be at their clients' by ten thirty at the latest, and it was already almost ten. They'd never make it.

"Allie," she shouted, pushing herself out of bed. Gah, her mouth felt like she'd been licking dirt. Probably should have taken the extra five minutes to brush her teeth before collapsing into bed. "We're late. Get up!"

She repeated herself twice more while stripping out of yesterday's

clothes and pulling on new ones. A shower would have to wait, unfortunately. The Farmers lived on the other side of town, sometimes
twenty minutes away, depending on traffic. Besides, they were
supposed to be repairing a porch swing in the front and installing a
new sump pump in their basement. What good would a shower do her
now when she was just going to get gross again.

By the time she left her room to wash her face and finally brush the
film from her teeth, she heard Allie rustling in her room.

"This is bull, Dee! I want you to know that! We should be resched-
uling." Allie popped her head out of her room, hair literally standing at
all angles. "We are not in the right frame of mind to do," she waved a
hand, "whatever we're supposed to do today."

"I know." Dee cranked the hot water faucet, waiting for the water
to hit a degree somewhere above freezing. "But we can't risk it. What
happens when people start hearing about this? The whole city probably already knows. It wasn't like the cops were subtle."

"Who cares? People know us. They aren't stupid. No one is going
to believe we had anything to do with all the disappearing kids' stuff."

She wanted to argue, but her mouth was full of foaming spit and
there wasn't a point. Allie was just making her opinion known. She'd
get dressed and be ready to go, same as Dee. She had lofty plans, and
lofty plans required money. Allie had never turned down work, no
matter how beneath her it might have once been.

From downstairs, Leander called for both pets and let the roommates know he was making coffee.

Slowly, Dee leaned out the bathroom door, toothpaste dotting her
chin to see Allie still leaning out her bedroom.

Allie mouthed *He's making coffee* and wiggled her eyebrows.

Dee blushed to her roots and ducked back into the bathroom. She
hadn't forgotten Leander spent the night, exactly, but she also kind of
assumed he'd be gone already. After all, he also owned a business and,
presumably, had stuff to do, things to repair, old ladies to flirt with. She
hadn't expected him to stay long enough to make coffee and feed the
pets.

"Hey, Lee," Allie shouted from her room. "Can you also make us
breakfast? I'm freaking starving."

"I would," he shouted back as Dee's blush changed from light rose red to a deep brick. "But you two have nothing in your fridge. Seriously, your mayo is expired. Who has expired mayo? That junk lasts forever."

Dee picked up the pace, scrubbing at her face, smearing on face cream, and quickly braiding her hair. She didn't know why, but something propelled her downstairs before Allie said something that really caught his attention. Not that Allie would be to blame, of course, but men noticed her. She was blonde and lovely and the freaking guy from the bakery paid her portion of the bail even though Allie would never give him the time of day. Men loved her, and Dee didn't think she could handle seeing that adoration on Leander's face. Not for her friend, anyway. She'd accepted it would happen with some gorgeous woman or other, and that was fine. She would deal. But, not Allie. That would be too much, especially after the last twenty-four hours.

"Hey, shortcake." Leander stood in her kitchen, bent slightly forward to set the pet's water dish on the floor. He wore nothing but a white tee shirt stretched tight over his expansive back and a pair of blue boxer briefs, which was not okay. A man should not feel comfortable enough to go around in his underwear. "I just put some water into the machine. Haven't added the grounds yet."

"I'll do it," she said quickly, marching over to the machine. "You go put on pants."

He hummed as he passed her, patting her on the head, oblivious as always to her state of mind. "Make it strong. We're all going to need it today. Oh, and, I think you should take Kansas with you, just in case."

Which she did, because arguing about it would take too much time.

Leander offered to take them to pick up Bertha, assuring Dee that Kansas would be fine inside the secured dog crate he kept in the truck bed, because you never knew when you'd run into a dog that needs a rescue. They had all finally made it out of the house, when they were intercepted.

Their landlady didn't come around often. Usually, she swanned in if they complained about anything that they weren't easily able to fix themselves. Then she would show up, breathless and complaining about how they were the "repair girls," shouldn't they be able to take care of the minor household issues all by themselves? She'd deduct it from their rent, of course, etc. etc. Except, she'd never deducted the minor repairs off the rent, so why would they ever believe she would do so for anything major?

She was handsome in a way with her thick black hair and bright red lips. She was ageless as far as Dee was concerned, unable to ever nail the lady down on a decade, much less an exact age.

She had just opened her mouth, just started to say, "Well, well, I didn't expect—"

When Kansas whirled from the tree he'd been sniffing and launched into a snarling growl, the hair rising along his spine.

"Goodness," Mrs. Thorne gasped, which sent him from snarling to straight up barking, his canines on full display, the deep-throated nature of his barking causing the landlady to stumble backwards.

"Kansas, stop," Dee snapped just as Leander put himself between the landlady and Dee's snarling dog. "I'm so sorry," she apologized. "He's never like that."

Except, maybe when someone came into the yard to dump a body. She threw Allie a quick glance to see her same thought reflected in her friend's eyes. Allie had already been upstairs when Leander mentioned Kansas scaring away the kidnapper or whoever put the kid in their yard. But they both knew Kansas was a good judge of character. It was why he always growled whenever the creepy old man walked past their house.

Except, he'd never growled at Mrs. Thorne before.

"Well, I would hope not." Mrs. Thorne stood just outside their yard on the sidewalk, a hand to her heart.

"Is there something you need, Mrs. Thorne?" Allie asked, stepping around Leander, making herself the target of the conversation. It was no secret Mrs. Thorne didn't like them. She'd been a pain since they moved in; texts when rent was due every month, even though they'd never been late, mentions of even the slightest complaint by their neighbors. The dog was loud once at night, Allie's bedroom window was open and she talked all night long to who knew who, there were people constantly coming and going. All lies. They were some of the most self-contained people Dee knew. But at least she was mostly cordial to Dee. The same could not be said for Allie's interactions with the landlady.

"Well, yes, dear," Mrs. Thorne said, brushing her long black hair over both shoulders. "Of course, there is. I wouldn't be here other-wise." Her mouth twisted into a slightly menacing snarl. "The rent is due, you know, and I'm not sure if either of you are aware, but your contract expired last month. I'm unsure whether I want to renew, especially considering what happened two nights ago."

Dee balked. Despite Mrs. Thorne's objections to them, they were model tenants. There weren't even any stray holes in the walls. Every-thing they hung, they hung with sticky hooks that wouldn't hurt the paint or the plaster. There were no scratches or dings on the hardwood floor. Dee was even considering putting a new coat of polyurethane down in the living room just because she wanted to see the flooring shine.

"That wasn't our fault," Allie snapped.

Mrs. Thorne narrowed her eyes. "Wasn't it? Hmm." She inspected the pointed red nails on her right hand, and then, without any warning, the hand shot out, grabbing Allie around the wrist, yanking her forward. "Where did you get this? Did you find it?" She pinched a charm on Allie's bracelet. "This rose charm is mine."

Allie jerked away. "It's not a rose, and it's mine." She thrust the wrist behind her back and Dee couldn't help but notice there wasn't a rose anywhere to be found. Did Mrs. Thorne need glasses?

There was a fun pair of silver slippers, though those didn't fit in with Allie's vibe. Allie was about glamour, not demure slippers. To be fair, they were probably based on some excessively expensive slippers. Gah. Why was she fixating on a stupid charm? There were bigger issues at hand.

Mrs. Thorne glared for a few seconds, her eyes hard as marble, before Leander broke the tension with a heavy sigh. "Ladies, if you're ready?"

"I am," Dee exclaimed, dragging Kansas to Lee's truck, urging him up into the bed and then inside the crate.

"We still need to talk, girls. I'm not comfortable renting to suspected criminals."

"We are not criminals," Allie snapped, completely unable to hide her true feelings for the landlady. "That's absurd, and you know it."

"Well, anyone with a body by their trash bins must be a little suspicious, don't you think?"

"No," both Allie and Dee said, catching each other's eyes again.

Did anyone besides the police know where the body was found? Was it in the paper? How would Mrs. Thorne know that?

Unless...

But, no. Mrs. Thorne was a nosy, slightly neglectful, and heavy-handed landlady. Dogs were not without fault. Kansas could be having a bad day, especially after spending the night alone. He wasn't used to it, since Dee never spent all night outside the house. She may have just surprised him, and he'd reacted badly. It did not mean anything.

Probably.

"What a drama queen." Allie exhaled as they climbed into Lee's truck, slamming the door shut. "Can you believe her?"

"How did she know where the boy was found?" Dee asked.

Allie shook her head, pulling the seat belt over her chest. "I wouldn't put it past that bitch to have cameras in our house."

Dee knew Allie was joking, but that didn't stop the goosebumps that rose along her arms. Someone had put a target on them, and she had no idea who it was or how to find out.

Chapter Seven

CANCEL COUTURE

llie watched Dee and Leander disappear into Black Forest Bakery, her stomach twisting with familiar dread. Every time she clawed her way toward something better, the past dragged her back down. Not just back—deeper. Finding that boy had cracked something open, something she had buried years ago. Now the truth leaked out like poison.

"It's not your fault," she whispered her therapist's mantra, inhaling deeply. Her exhale carried no relief. "It was an accident."

The lie tasted bitter. What happened back then wasn't an accident —it might not have been her fault, but she certainly wasn't blameless. Allison had made choices. One of those choices had cost her everything.

Still, Allie repeated it, and a few other affirmations, until the words felt real, and she was no longer concentrating on the past.

"Get your shit together, Allie. You got to face Mr. Purrkins or Reuben. Whatever. He's going to want something from you. They always do." She hesitated outside a little longer. Allie loathed owing anyone anything, especially a broke bakery clerk—or at least she had thought he was broke. Reuben Sourire—what a ridiculous name!— was a volunteer? Who had time or energy for all of that? Didn't he know society was collapsing? Probably had some sort of savior complex.

Mentally girded by these thoughts, Allie pushed ahead and through the door. She didn't expect to find Dee crumpled on the floor with Leander crouched next to her. Nor did she expect tiny Mrs. Leckermaul, looking like she'd had more work done, fanning Dee with a newspaper. She had no idea those things were still around. Reuben was also there on Dee's other side, offering her a bottle of water.

She shook her head, also shaking from her momentary shock from the scene. She rushed over. "Dee? Are you all right?"

"Well, of course I don't believe it!" Leckermaul said overly loudly, shoving the newspaper in Allie's face. "It's a shame that someone is treating you girls so. You're the real victims here..."

Ringing in her ears drowned out the rest of what the baker said, as Allie saw a screenshot of her gaming and an Instagram profile photo taken from the Jill of All Trades business's page. The headline was too stupid for words, the article was all speculation, but her username exposed next to her real name made her blood run cold. "Streaming Sensation Allegedly a Suspect in Sueños Del Mar's ongoing Child Abduction Investigation."

Her mouth went dry as if someone stuffed cotton in it, as she skimmed the article. The freaking police leaked that they were their prime suspects, and that they were out on bail. Was that even legal? The journalist was some hack named Alan Lemming. Hand to her throat, she gasped, "Water."

Her whole world narrowed to the bottle touching her lips. She grabbed the bottle and chugged. Instead of refreshing, the cool liquid went down poorly. She coughed and sputtered all over. A gentle hand rubbed her back as the other snatched the bottle from her hands.

"It's okay. Everything is going to be okay," Sourire said in a calm, steady tone.

Gaining her composure, she glared at him. He returned her glare with a grin, lighting up his stupid handsome face. *What was there to smile about?*

Needing space, she disentangled herself from him. "No. It is not. I do nothing but work and try to live a better life, and someone has dumped this crap on my doorstep. My do-gooder best friend is accused of being a criminal. How can any of this be okay?"

"Nothing lasts forever. Not even bad times."

The words carried weight, like he knew exactly what kind of bad times she'd survived. She turned away, watching Dee accept Leckermaul's offerings - coffee, pastries, sympathy that felt too calculated.

Leander opened the door for them.

"Message me on our private chat," Reuben called after her.

Allie made no promises. Talking was the last thing she wanted to do with Reuben Sourire.

~

*L*eander dropped the Jills of All Trades and their equipment at their first job of the day.

He eyed the house with undue suspicion. His gaze swung to Dorseigh. "You sure this is a good idea?"

Dee had to assure him several times she could do it. Allie just nodded along, not that Leander paid her any attention. She didn't mind. Reuben had given her too much.

Her friend turned to the house, determination on her face. This bolstered Allison. If her friend could be strong, so could she. They needed the money. Guilty people hid in the shadows. The innocent went about their lives. Right?

They fell into their routine. Thirty minutes into the clean, the owner of the house burst through the door. He was a tall man with a generous build that middle age and prosperity provided. His eyebrows lowered angrily. "What are you doing here?"

Allie swallowed down the fear the accusation in his tone had risen and waved the vacuum wand. "Um? What we do every week." The words came out sharp, defensive. She'd meant to be flippant.

Dee cut her a sharp look and then smiled at the client. "We're here for our scheduled clean. Did you cancel?"

His round face flushed red all the way to the collar of his polo shirt. "Yes. Yes, I did! Didn't you get my message?"

The two women exchanged glances. Neither had checked their phones. Dee shook her head. "Sorry. No."

He held out his hand, making a grabbing motion. "Contract terminated, effective immediately. Keys to my house."

The keys shook in Dee's grip as she handed them over. She held herself together until they got outside, but tears traced silent paths down her cheeks as they waited with their equipment—standing among the pieces of the life they'd built, watching it crumble.

"Hey, there's a mess in my kitchen," the man shouted from his porch.

Dee's gaze swung in his direction, confusion limning her features. Allison wiped her cheeks, turned and shrugged, "Not our problem."

Their former client harrumphed and slammed the door behind him.

"I might have accidentally opened the dustbin of the vacuum on the clean floor when I went to grab the mop," Allie admitted, spreading her palms at her partner's confused face. "We were in such a rush to get out; I had no time to clean it up."

Dee's laugh caught on a sob as she wiped her eyes. "It couldn't be helped. Hope he doesn't fire us." Her smile twisted. "Wait. Too late."

Allie managed a weak laugh, but sobriety settled quickly. "Should I check the messages, or do you want to?"

"We should both look." Dee pulled out her phone with trembling fingers. "Whatever's waiting, we face it together."

The words hit her like a physical blow. Together. That's how they'd survived everything else—the secrets, the pain, the past that haunted them both. But this time felt different. This time, her secrets might not just destroy her, but take Dee down too. She pulled out her own phone, dreading what waited on the screen. In this town, bad news traveled faster than truth.

～

*H*eartbeat thrumming in his ears, he scented the air. Two odors, both familiar, filled his nostrils. One was delicious and so, so tempting, even in this form. A large, satisfied smile crossed his lips. He'd found her. It had only taken a half an hour prowling the town and he was proud of his hunting skills.

Crawling, the rough material of the shingles scraped against the fur of his belly. His claws found purchase as he slinked across the roof, careful to go unnoticed by the two women below. Should either catch a glimpse of a striped tomcat watching them, they would grow concerned and attempt a rescue. He wouldn't tolerate that and would have to claw and bite his way to freedom. Helping others was who they were. That's how he *knew* they were innocent of all accusations.

That and he'd caught the scent of malicious magic on the comatose boy. The same nefarious magic that had clung to someone else. He wanted to turn her in but good luck explaining she smelled wrong to the police. Neither of these women ever smelled of foul spellwork, and he doubted they even knew it existed.

They were as unaware as everyone else about the why of it.

Still, he couldn't help but purr as he watched them hover over their phones. Golden California sunlight glinted off her platinum hair. She squinted at her screen. He inhaled deeply, with his mouth open so he could scent her feelings. Her distress tainted her amber and jasmine blossom odor with a pungent tang.

How would he push her in the right direction without revealing more?

His feline eyes caught on something glittering on her wrist, and he couldn't help but want a closer inspection. He prowled down the slope of the roof to get a better look.

His ears twitched and he arched his back. A hiss escaped his lips when he caught sight of an item half remembered but he knew was foul. Angry at this form's instinctual response to Allie's danger, he cursed inwardly and scrambled out of sight as the duo looked up.

*A*llie glanced at Dee as her bestie plopped into the chair she'd rolled in from her own room.

"Are you sure you're okay with this?"

Her roomie's cheeks flushed. She had the wholesome, girl next door vibe going for her. Her looks would give them a ton of views.

Conversely, Allie knew she looked ... expensive. Something she both tailored to the life she wanted and was raised to be. There was a time she rebelled against the idea of wealth and privilege, and still a part of her hated the Mrs. Thornes of the world, but living as a poor worker bee in a podunk town ... well, it gave a girl perspective. The world wasn't going to change despite what the online community thought. No one was going to dismantle the system. It was all for likes and shares, just like those who claimed to want to go back to something that never existed. The polarizing was on purpose. Keep them separated so they look anywhere but up.

Dee wrung her hands. "We need money for Thorne, and we need answers, so I have to be okay. Right?"

She swallowed hard. Thorne hated Allie specifically, but she also loved having her under her thumb. Allie wished she could assure Dee of this. Instead, she put her hand over Dee's churning fingers, stilling them.

Her friend lifted her eyes—red rimmed but not tearing up yet. If Dee cried, Allie might just lose it, too.

"We do, but I got you." She managed a grin, touched her chest, and gave her best throaty laugh. In a sultry voice, she crooned, "Streaming is what I do, babe. Streaming is what I live for."

Her roomie snorted. "These allegations have brought out your inner villain."

"You have no idea, darling." Allie winked. The oppressive weight on her chest that made even breathing hard lifted a bit as she joined her friend in a genuine chuckle. Sobering, she flipped on her monitor and brought up the live stream video site, logging in and turning on her camera without starting the video and chat yet. After adjusting the overhead mic once more so Dee would be in full view she said, "Last chance to back out."

Dee shook her head, but her fingers gripped her coffee mug tightly enough that the knuckles turned white. She furrowed her pale eyebrows. "Do they really give you money to just watch you game?"

"To watch me game, shop, pet my cat, and sleep."

"Must be nice to be gorgeous while you do normal shit," she

muttered.

Allie gripped Dee's chin and forced her friend to look at them on the monitor. "This woman owns her business, she works hard, gives all of herself to everyone else, and looks every bit as beautiful as I do while she does it. The only problem is that she doesn't see it. When she does, she'll be the baddest baddie around." With that, she let go and let it sink in.

Scowling, Dee rubbed her chin. "You know what I mean. I'm not glamorous."

"Which is perfect. I'm not everyone's cup of tea. No one is."

While her friend chewed on her lip, likely mulling over what she'd said, Allie nodded at her and went live. A little green light at the top of the monitor notified them that they were being recorded. Dee stiffened. Deciding she was a lost cause; Allie tucked her blonde hair behind her ears and brought up some Sueños Del Mar community chats on the other screen.

It didn't take long before her stomach sank. Someone had posted the article. The feed went rabid. Accusations flew, each more ridiculous than the last. Their business was brought up. Her sudden appearance at the high school in junior year with no one knowing where she came from or ever seeing her parents came up as suspicious. The conspiracies flew.

Her heart raced. What if people started digging into that? The detective might.

"Allie," Dee's voice held a note of distress. "You better take a look at this."

She had to shake her head to break the downward spiral that she'd rapidly descended into, and she focused on the live stream monitor. There was a notification that she'd been banned from the website temporarily for reported misconduct.

"What the heck?"

Dee swallowed hard and then spoke in rapid fire succession, "The messages came in so fast. The accusations were so crazy. They even accused you of playing pre-recorded videos on your live so that you'd have an alibi. The only person who defended you—Mr. Purrkins?—got banned. We're in serious trouble, Allison."

Chapter Eight

WOUNDS OLD AND NEW

he nightmare was never clear enough to last, visually. Once Dee opened her eyes, the dream images dissolved to vapors, leaving only the emotions. The fear and confusion. The loss. Sometimes she woke up believing she was on the verge of dying of thirst. A few years after the dreams started, she made sure there was always a full glass of water on her nightstand table, freshly refilled before she climbed into bed. Except for after getting home at four in the morning and the stress of the day, she'd forgotten to refresh the water beside her bed. It was two days old and stale.

She didn't think about it when she woke up gasping, the tapestry of threads holding the old nightmare together unraveling as they always did. Fear. Confusion. Isolation. Death. And thirst. Parched, like she hadn't found moisture in days. Out of habit, she reached for the glass and chugged, cringing at the staleness, but swallowed anyway. When you were on the verge of death, you'd drink almost anything.

Beside Dee, Kansas whined, nuzzling closer to her, his lean body pressed against hers. Usually, she'd reassure him with a pat, letting him know she was fine, everything was fine, just a silly dream. But this dream didn't dissipate like before. She sat in her bed, in her room, in a California house, and saw the swirling wind kicking up dust. She squeezed her eyes shut, but it was still there, the wind moving in a fury across the flat land, whipping her hair into tangles as her father ran towards the cellar.

"No," she whispered into the dark, giving her head a firm shake. "*No*."

She shut out the memories as firmly as her father had shut the root cellar door. She wouldn't go back there. There were too many things happening in her present life to fall into the trap of her past.

Finally, after long minutes of wrangling her heartbeat under control and thinking of more pleasant things—Leander in boxer briefs leapt to mind, but she also shoved that aside—she lay back down. Running a hand over Kansas's sleek side, she finally fell into a doze, just deep enough to make her groggy, when her phone's alarm started its ritualistic chiming right at seven in the morning. What was the point of getting up in the morning if there wasn't anywhere to go? No jobs, anyway.

Of course, that didn't mean she didn't have a life outside of the business. Sure, she usually picked up a few odd jobs in any downtime. Allie had her streaming, and Dee had her need to fix. She mowed the neighbor's yard when his arthritis was acting up. She fixed brownies for the church potlucks, even though she wasn't a member. She donated time to the community center, picking up trash and sometimes even mentoring the kid of a single parent. She knew what it was like to lose one or both parents, which made her uniquely qualified to spend some time with them, to let them know life goes on.

Lying there, she tried to think of something else to do. Something for *herself*.

There was nothing.

How could there be nothing?

"Dee," Allie screeched from her room. "Look at this absolute shit!"

Dee stayed paralyzed in her bed for a few seconds, torn between remaining ignorant or knowledgeable to whatever Allie was worked up about first thing in the morning. With a groan, she rolled out of bed and stumbled down the hall, Kansas at her heels.

"What is it," she asked around a yawn, falling onto the bed beside her first-thing-in-the-morning disheveled friend. It was the *only* time Allison looked disheveled.

"This!" Her phone was shoved into Dee's face.

On it—once she moved it back a fair distance from her face—she saw a text from Mrs. Thorne. Oh yeah. They forgot to send her payment yesterday. The woman was threatening them with imminent eviction if they didn't pay immediately. Which, fine. They did need to pay rent. But, also, Dee wanted *in writing* that if they paid, they would be guaranteed the full month.

"Tell her that if she agrees to let us stay until at least the end of the month without threatening us again, then we'll pay. Otherwise," Dee shrugged, feigning a nonchalance that no one who knew her would believe. "I guess we'll find a new place to live."

"Like hell," Allie mumbled, snatching back her phone. "I will eat her up if she tries to kick us out."

With a snort, Dee rolled off the bed, heading downstairs for coffee and to tend to the pets. Once Allie followed a quarter of an hour later, Dee had already opened her laptop and found how she was going to spend her day.

"What're you doing?" Allie slid into the chair across from her after putting water into the electric kettle.

"Well, I figured if we were going to be accused of kidnapping, we should at least know what we're up against." Dee shrugged. The idea had come to her while she stood at the back door, a full trash bag in one hand, her other on the doorknob. Outside, two steps down and three forward, sat the bins, yellow tape strung around them. She'd stared at that tape for a very long time. Or, what felt like a very long time. Probably only a few minutes, though, since the coffee was still percolating, and Allie had come downstairs by the time she shook herself out of her thoughts. "Shouldn't the police have turned our house upside down?" She looked from her screen to Allie. "I mean, they found a body here. Shouldn't they be like, I don't know, processing the scene or something? They processed the scene at the house of the kidnapped kids. They kept the parents out for over a week. But here? Nothing. That doesn't make sense."

"Are you seriously asking me? Because I'm a lot of things, but a true crime girlie is not one of them."

"I know, Allison, but there was a crime, and evidence was planted *here,* and they haven't even been through our house. Shouldn't they have been through our house?"

Allison shrugged. "Maybe? Maybe they'll do it now that they've charged us?"

Dee shook her head. "No, I don't think that's how it works. I think they should have kicked us out of our house the night you found the kid. They should have been going through our house and yard at the very least, looking for evidence. It's just not right. This entire thing is not right."

Drumming her fingers on the table, Allie gave one slow nod. "Okay. So, what are you doing?"

"Reading." Dee turned her laptop around so Allie could see the headline at the top of the screen. "Did you know that only some of the kids are still missing and that the ones who have been returned, all of them are in comas? For some reason, the papers only state they have been found and are under observation, but I found a blog post that says they have seen the returned kids and they're all unconscious. You want to know something else weird?"

"Lay it on me."

"The Chroner's little boy, Jack, was one of the taken."

"Who the hell are the Chroners?" Allie stood to fix her tea.

"The Chroners live three streets over. They are renters. Want to take a wild guess who their landlady is?"

"Shut. Up." Allie spun, scalding water sloshing everywhere. Rabbit hissed as a drop or two landed on his bare skin before he bolted from the room.

"Yeah, and," Dee gave her friend a grim smile, "none of her tenants have kind things to say about her. Some reporter wrote a story about rent hikes a few years ago, and Mrs. Thorne was one of the main villains of the story. Surprise, surprise."

"What does all this mean, though? How does this help us?"

"I don't know, yet. But maybe we should find out? Our lives might be on the line, we can't afford a lawyer, our clients are abandoning us. We have to do something."

"What do you want to do?"

After jotting down a few lines on the notepad they generally used for groceries, Dee said, "I think we should talk to some of these tenants. See if they've noticed anything weird. Maybe even the Chroners." Her stomach twisted at the thought, but she'd do it, because it was a better idea than just hiding in their house and hoping the missing kids would be found or the unconscious wake up, clearing them of any guilt.

"Tell me more."

While Dee worked on the list of names and addresses, Allie wrote an appeal to have her streaming services returned. Dee wouldn't admit this out loud, but she didn't think talking to most of the names on her list would do any good. Only the Chroners mattered. Regardless, she would go down each of the five. Even if neither of them had any idea what they were doing, it was time to learn. She had very little faith that outside help was coming.

After a sufficient amount of caffeine was consumed, they headed out on foot. Two of the houses were vacant, either because they moved somewhere else in town or left altogether. Which was rare in Sueños. People didn't seem to leave. Like any seaside town, there were tourists, but with no hotels and few bed-and-breakfast places, visitors didn't tend to stay long. The residents though? Many of them were lifers.

Of the two renters who weren't the Chroners, they didn't learn much more than they already knew: Thorne rarely fixed issues, she started threatening eviction beginning at noon on the day rent was due, and her husband was a jumpy, creepy man. One thing they did say was that she'd been sniffing around a lot more over the last few weeks.

Ever since the kids started going missing.

They purposefully left the Chroners for last. Mostly because their house was the furthest away, but also because they were afraid of what would happen. They didn't know the family—which, if Dee had known sooner, she would have pointed out to Doyle with his assertions that they were connected to *all* the missing kids—had never worked for them or even seen them around town. According to the article about their missing son, they'd moved in less than a year ago. It was possible the parents wouldn't know who Dee and Allie were. Then again, the town loved gossip. She had to assume everyone had heard, and the parent of a missing child would not be inclined to talk to them.

They stood on the sidewalk in front of the house next door to the Chroners and watched. The street was lined with older model cars, even though it was the middle of a workday. Which could mean either a lot of the residents of this street worked remote or didn't work normal business hours. Dee would have preferred the street to be empty. She didn't want a whole host of witnesses if the Chroners decided to scream at them.

"Are we really going to do this?" Allie asked, playing with the charm bracelet she always seemed to wear these days.

As it was the day before, Dee's eyes traveled to the little charm of shoes. "I don't... I mean, yes."

"I guess we walked all this way."

It had taken them around twenty minutes from the last house to this one. It would take nearly half an hour to walk home. It was more like a stroll than a hike, but Dee knew what Allie meant. The mental toll of walking up to a house where a parent might believe their child's kidnapper was outside the door was much more draining than the walk.

"I wish we had someone else to do this," Allie added, squaring her shoulders. "Come on. Let's get it over with."

If any luck dwelled in either of them, they used it all up when they knocked on the Chroner's door. Kelly Chroner answered right away. A slight woman with dark hair a couple days beyond greasy and dark purple bruises under her hazel eyes, she stood in the open door of her rental home regarding them warily.

"Do you have a minute to talk?" Dee asked gently, both unwilling and unable to push the woman too quickly.

Kelly Chroner nodded. She was home for only a few minutes, she said, stopping in to grab a few things before heading back to the hospital. Her son Jack was in the hospital, but she didn't elaborate further. That was fine. They all knew why Jack Chroner was in the hospital. Even though he'd been the first child found, he hadn't woken up.

Allie, as if knowing by some unspoken communication, hid their true purpose. She told the mother they were following up on the old news story. She asked if things were any better for renters. Dee could not see how they could be. She wouldn't go so far as to call the Thornes slum lords, but it was near enough. She and Allie's house was amazing, of course and since she hadn't lived anywhere else in her adult life besides Sueños Del Mar, she couldn't be positive, but it was unlikely she'd be able to afford their home in most parts of California. Maybe even in most parts of any state. She'd looked at houses in other communities, and it was always shocking how little they paid. Still, most of the houses they'd visited were nothing special. The further they traveled from their own neighborhood, the dingier the houses became. Chipped paint and mildew-slicked shingles, broken driveways and missing shutters were all increasingly familiar sights within only a fifteen-minute walk from their own neighborhood. Who knew what state their darling little Victorian would be in without the two of them there to keep it pristine.

Sueños Del Mar should be one of those places full of the wealthy, which there were plenty of wealthy citizens. Around the bay and a few streets back into the downtown area was mostly storefronts and water-related businesses. Further back, once you were beyond the downtown with its boutiques and cafes and city government buildings, the quality of homes and residents declined. While their street was still solidly middle class, rarely any of the homes were owned, the rest of the residents were renters with few as invested as Dee and Allie in the upkeep of their home. Nothing egregious, but paint was chipped and never touched up, gutters would overflow, weeds were allowed to spout in the sidewalk cracks.

Of course, once you made it to the southwest edge of town, there was the gated neighborhood on the hill, where the people did all own their homes. People on the hill had amazing views of the ocean from the comfort of their expansive front yards. She supposed they might be able to keep an eye on their yachts and houseboats, their cruisers and sailboats. Dee knew very little about the people who lived on the hill. They had their own post office and mini-downtown area, their own private school. The hill community was nearly as large as the rest of Sueños. They kept to themselves, unless they came down to harass their renters, ala Mrs. Thorne.

Kelly Chroner couldn't comment on whether things were better, of course, because they'd only recently moved in. She and her husband worked service jobs—she was a waitress in one of the downtown cafes and he was a tech for the local internet provider—and tended to move whenever the rent was raised. As it was, they were already keeping an eye out for somewhere else to live. The rent was okay, but the landlady, she told them, seemed to always be around, bothering them about one thing or another. Were they minding the irises in the backyard? She didn't want the new family to accidentally mow them down. Did the dogwood bloom in the spring? How long did it hold the blooms? She would be standing in their front yard, staring at the pine trees, checking for pests. Kelly Chroner thought it was bizarre the landlady had such a fixation on the plant life around their house. Which, considering Mrs. Thorne hadn't asked them even once about the foliage around their own home, Dee understood. But, also, Mrs. Thorne was a little weird with her bright red lips and her sleek black hair. Dee was always reminded of a storybook character, though never one in particular. Her mind always seemed to blank when she thought about it too long.

Dee asked, "What did she do when she found out your son was one of the missing children?"

After a few seconds of confused silence, Kelly Chroner asked back, "What do you mean? What should she have done?"

Neither Dee nor Allie had a good answer.

"Um, just, you know, was she supportive?"

"Oh." Kelly Chroner gripped the door frame where she stood answering their questions, having the good sense to not invite two strangers into her home. "I don't remember. I don't think so, though, no. She did come by once after the police found him." She paused for a second, staring off, remembering the day, Dee guessed. "She called, I think. Said something about not letting the police tear up the yard. I didn't really think about it at the time, you know? There was too much going on. Why would I care about the yard?"

They left shortly after, unsure if they accomplished anything or not other than getting some steps in. They already knew Mrs. Thorne was not a kind woman, but other than digging around in someone else's yard, there wasn't much they could do to point the blame elsewhere.

Dee chewed a nail on the way home, her thoughts churning with what else they could do. After reading about the abducted children, she had a vague idea of where the three boys were found. Well, vague idea about two of the three, anyway. McGregor Park near the thick wooded area that surrounded the landside of town, and the back parking lot near the hospital. The third one ... well, that was her own yard, of course.

What good did that do her? What was she going to do? Go to the other places where the kids were found and search for clues? Hope to find a note that listed both who did it and why?

"You know what we need?" she finally asked once they were back home.

"You mean other than a one-way ticket out of this town?" Allie asked back, pulling off her shoes and heading toward the kitchen.

"A lawyer, Allie. We need to get a lawyer."

"They're going to assign us one. A *free* one."

"I asked for a lawyer after we were arrested, and I never saw one. Did you?" She followed Allie, Kansas at her side. She'd have to remember not to mention their stroll about town to Lee. He'd probably berate her for not taking Kansas with them. She nearly snorted. *Berate.* More like gently chide. Dee was pretty sure only passionate people berated. And if Lee was passionate about anyone, she had yet to witness it.

"They have to give us one, don't they? Isn't that the law?"

They stood on opposite sides of the table, Allie with her back to the sink and Dee with hers to the small writing desk that was conveniently covered in mixing bowls. A couple of the cabinets had started sagging a few months ago, and, surprise, surprise, Thorne hadn't made any move toward fixing those. She'd probably suggest the girls do it. Which, yeah, they probably would, because houses with sagging cabinets could not be considered pristine.

"I guess." Dee threw her hands up, frustration and interrupted sleep finally catching up with her. "But how do we go about it? Do we call the police station and ask them to get the lawyer I asked for two days ago?"

"Well—"

"And who even knows if the lawyer will be worth anything? Aren't public defenders usually pretty bad?"

"Are you asking me if I—"

"We should get a real lawyer. Someone who is *paid* to defend us."

"Are you going to let me talk or what?"

"I have three hundred dollars in my checking account. How much do you have?"

Allie flew away from the counter, slashing her hand through the air, eyes wide, chin up. She practically vibrated. Dee could swear she even grew a few inches. "No. That is *not* what I'm spending my money on. I'll take my chances with the public servant."

"Allie! This is important! This is our life, we can't trust just anyone. We need to—"

Allie jumped in to cut Dee off this time, "We can. It'll be fine, Dee. A public defender will do their job. We can't afford a freaking lawyer."

"Then we'll get a loan." Dee crossed her arms, jaw set, defiant. She was never defiant. Not anymore. The last time she was, her parents died.

"From who?" Allie shouted, turning toward the sink, refilling the electric kettle, and grabbing a box of the loose-leaf tea she ordered every month from a company located all the way in England. "Are your aunt and uncle suddenly wealthy? Have they been squirreling away pennies? Where would we get a loan?"

Dee knew she shouldn't say what was on the tip of her tongue. There were some things, some topics, that were avoided. An unspoken agreement that this or that was off-limits. She'd always respected Allie's conversation boundaries because she had topics of her own she would rather keep locked up, to never face. But, the time for tact was gone, lost to circumstances two days ago.

"What about your family?"

Allie spun, sputtering. "My family? *My family*? Are you out of your mind? I am not," she sucked in a breath, blue eyes going cold. "We're not doing this, Dee. We can't afford a lawyer. We'll take what they give us."

"I—"

"No. Absolutely not. End of conversation."

Kansas barked two seconds before the doorbell rang. They both stopped, a flash of fear rippling through Dee's brain.

Allie leaned to the left, looking down the hall, and rolled her eyes. "Judging by the outline through the curtain, I'd say it's Lee."

"Oh." Returning Bertha, probably.

Sure enough, he stood on the other side of the door, holding Dee's keyring between two meaty fingers. "Hey, shortcake. Got your ride all fixed."

"Thanks." She snatched the keys away from him, shoving them in her pocket before stepping out and shutting the door behind her. "Send me the bill." She jumped down the steps, heading toward the sidewalk. She needed another walk. A quiet walk where she could clear her head and come up with a plan. If they couldn't get a lawyer, if neither of them was able to scrounge up the funding, then they had to have a plan.

"Where you headed?" Leander fell easily into step next to her.

"I don't know. Away." She stopped and faced him. "Alone."

Two thick eyebrows rose on his stupidly handsome face. "You think that's a good idea?"

Dee snorted. "Yeah, I do. I'm fine." She took two steps, stopped, and looked back at him. "I appreciate you bringing Bertha. Send me the bill, please."

When he kept following her, she stopped again to face him. "What are you doing?"

"Well, I'm walking home. I drove your truck over," he shrugged.

Oh. Duh. Of course.

She mumbled an apology, waiting for him to take the two steps to catch up to her. They walked in silence for a block before he said, "Mind if I ask what's got your dander up?"

"My dander?" She scoffed.

"Yeah, shortcake. You're all puffed up like an angry cat."

"I am not puffed up," Dee cried indignantly.

"You know what I mean. Did something happen with the police or Thorne?"

Dee sighed, unable to stay angry in his presence. He had been nothing but helpful, there wasn't a reason to take out her sudden bad mood on him.

"We need a lawyer, and we can't afford one. Allie wants to use a public defender, but I want someone else. Someone good. Someone who will help us."

"Someone like that?" He nodded toward a bus stop bench with an advertisement of a smiling blonde lady and the words "free consultation" in all caps and below that "Susan Glenda, Attorney-at-Law". "Her ads are all over town. Maybe she can help."

Dee had seen that exact ad so many times, it had become background noise. But now, looking at Susan Glenda's smiling face, Dee felt just the tiniest glimmer of hope, like, yes, maybe this woman can help.

She pulled her phone out of her back pocket, dialed the listed number, and held her breath.

Chapter Nine

ROCK HARD BOTTOM PAWN STAR

*B*ertha started on the first try, her motor roaring like a lioness defending her pride. Guess Dee wasn't the only one with a thing for Leander's touch. But a working truck didn't solve Allie's bigger problems: she was irate, broke, and one wrong move from having her past exposed to everyone in this suffocating town.

Maybe Dee was right. Her mother could sweep in and make this disappear like she had made everything else that inconvenienced her disappear before. No. Allie wasn't her daughter anymore. Her mother would let her rot in jail.

Anger flared in her chest, consuming the ache. How dare Dee suggest asking her parents for help? Dee knew what had happened. She knew there was no going back home. Not after everything.

She let muscle memory guide her through streets until she found herself outside Black Forest Bakery, the sweet aromas carrying an edge she'd never noticed before. Like something menacing lurking beneath sugar and spice.

It was all in her head. Everything felt like a threat now. She just needed to get out of the car, go in, and announce that she couldn't pay Reuben back, not yet anyway. Pride, something she thought she'd long lost, kept her ass firmly planted in the driver's seat.

Forearms and then a face appeared in the passenger window. The scent of baked goods sweetening the air and a cologne a baker-slash-volunteer firefighter shouldn't be able to afford wafted in her nostrils, unbidden. Unwanted. She would not inhale his scent. Not intentionally.

Allison gripped the steering wheel, eyes forward. There was no way she could meet his gaze. He'd been her online friend for a few years now, always having her back, but this was real life. He was no rebel, and she was no vigilante, avenging her dead family. Her relatives were alive and well. Unfortunately for them, so was she.

"You know," his voice held that silken warmth she remembered from late-night streams, "you can let go once the vehicle is in park."

She swallowed the knot in her throat.

"I can't pay you back," she managed. "Not yet."

"Don't worry about it, Wandergirl."

The username hit like a punch to the gut. Wandergirl was supposed to be her escape, her hero persona. Now it was just another thing this town had tainted. "Wandergirl doesn't exist anymore. My profile got banned."

He scratched his neck, blew out a breath that carried too much knowing. "I heard. Look—"

"Why would you post bail for me?" She glared at his stupidly perfect hair, his shadow-dark jaw. Everything about him felt like a beautiful lie.

His grin sparked something dangerous in her chest. "Because we're friends. I know you didn't take those kids. You know what it's like to be at someone's mercy."

"Because of the game?" A frisson of fear danced down her spine. Her secrets were locked tight, buried by money and influence. But Reuben spoke like he could see right through her walls. Like he *knew* her secrets. Between him and Doyle, Allison was sick of people seeming to know what she'd paid so dearly to be long, long over. She pulled on her mean girl armor. "That's pretend. What could you possibly know about me?"

"A lot more than you know about me." The saltiness in his tone spoke volumes of how he felt about it, too.

"Oh, really. Do you stalk me?" The accusation masked the fledgling worry that Reuben might actually be a digital stalker. The last thing she needed was a hacker digging into her past. That cloud already loomed over her constantly, and Dee asking her to beseech her parents for money only darkened it.

Something passed over his face—Surprise? Shock? Fear?—and then he shook his head as if shaking off the emotion. Reuben held up his hands. "Whoa! I'm not an internet stalker." With a broad gesture, he added, "Most people know each other here. You go around this town as if—as if, none of us matter. Like we're a stepladder to what you really want. But this is your town, too. People care about you. You only have to look beyond your mirror to see that."

The truth of it made the backs of her eyes sting with unshed tears. She thought about Leander and the clients who had, up until recently, treated Dee and her like family. The town turned on *Jills of All Trades* despite how much she and Dorseigh had done to make their lives better by fixing their things and cleaning their messes. The thought left a bitter taste in her mouth.

And, what did Reuben *really* know? He'd assumed she was stuck up just like everyone else did. She wasn't, even for all her caviar dreams. She'd never thought less of anyone without money. She had to leave, though. She had to do it in a way the people who'd made her life this bad wouldn't ever find her again.

Sometimes places held so much hurt that it became a palpable thing. A weight that presses on you and the only way you'll be free is to leave that albatross behind so you can breathe. As long as she stayed here, she'd have that damned cloud and the oppressive weight. A rich woman abroad could remain mysterious. Small towns had a way of steamrolling all the secrets out of you.

She gave herself a mental shake and blew out her breath. "I don't want to step on anyone. It's ... this isn't where I want to be. If I go to jail, the wrong person will go free and—" But, *I'll finally be punished for the terrible things I've done.*

"Then you should get a lawyer. The one they will appoint you won't let you leave."

She furrowed her brow. "What do you mean?"

Reuben looked both ways, opened the door and hopped into the truck. "Roll up your window."

Allie stared at him, confused.

"I'm going to say something controversial, and there are ears everywhere." He nodded toward the elderly man who scuffled across town every day on his morning walk. The old man waved and grinned. She and Reuben waved back. The old man's gaze landed on her arm, eyes and features, sharpening like an apex predator narrowing its gaze on prey.

A chill ran down the column of her spine as if someone had poured cold water down her back. Instinctively, she pulled her arm down against her belly, and covered it with her other arm. Reuben seemed to puff up a little bit, as if he was subconsciously aware of her fear and ready to pounce. All of it was ridiculous. All over an elderly man who was likely senile, not watching. His attention had got caught on her shiny bracelet. That's all.

The old man blinked as if waking and then resumed shuffling, bending over to retrieve what seemed to be an antique timepiece. A pocket watch that shimmered in the sunlight. The watch intrigued her, catching and holding her eye. Like a cat spotting a shiny moving object, she wanted to chase the glittering chain as he put it away, removing it from her sight. She knew that pocket watch. A glimmer of a memory sparked, and an uncanny sense that nothing was real washed over her.

"Are you all right there?" Reuben's voice cut into that feeling.

It took her a second to recover. She gripped the steering wheel, feeling the material. However, her eyes stayed on the old man. The urge to follow him and snatch his timepiece had a stranglehold on her. It wasn't like the feeling she had when she snatched something on the job. It was much, much worse. She blew out her breath and forced herself to look away from the elderly man and face Reuben.

"Yeah. He had an amazing timepiece. I'm into vintage pieces."

His gaze dipped to where she covered her arm, or more importantly, her rabbit charm. "So, I've noticed."

She fought to stop protectively covering her charm bracelet and placed her hands on the steering wheel again. "I'll pay you back soon."

He waved a dismissive hand. "You don't—"

"So, what were you going to say that was controversial?"

Reuben gave her a long look and then blew out his breath. "I don't blame you for wanting to leave. There's a lot not right here."

The uncanny sensation she got whenever she thought of just driving Bertha until the old truck ran out of gas surfaced. It was something she struggled with since high school.

"Ever notice that nobody talks about certain things? There's a very particular process to an arrest, to being questioned because laws dictate such things. You should have had a lawyer present and a right to call whomever you wish, for one. It's federal law. You got none of that. If I looked it up on the internet a few weeks ago, I'd find everything I needed to know about Miranda rights and due process. Now that I want to help you legally, I can't find anything."

"You're wrong. Information on the internet doesn't just disappear. Maybe you found a hoax site and it was taken down," she said, but it felt as if the words bubbled up on their own—as if she was supposed to say them like an actor delivering lines but she didn't have any true feelings associated with what she said. Her hand flew to her mouth. Horrified, Allie met Reuben's gaze.

His smile turned sharp, a sinister edge to it. Yet, she didn't fear him or his grin as much as the compulsion to say something she didn't mean. Reuben laughed, a deep rumbling purr.

"Get yourself a lawyer of your choosing. Make sure they have the same reaction."

He winked and slipped out of the car, leaving her in a more confused state than when she started.

~

*P*acing her bedroom, Allie stared at the letter "M" in her contacts with the caution one would use with a viper that could strike at any moment. One call could make this all disappear—or make everything so much worse. Her mother's influence could sweep away accusations, but it would come with chains. The same chains she'd broken at sixteen when they'd paid her to disappear. The mirror caught her movement, and she froze.

Her mother's face stared back—those same delicate features, large blue eyes, that distinctive platinum blonde hair. But where her mother wore Chanel and disdain, Allie had on jeans and a cute top. Accessible. Common. Everything her mother loathed.

The charm bracelet felt suddenly heavy on her wrist. Everyone who looked at it saw something different, something they wanted. Just like her mother had always seen what she wanted in Allie. Until she didn't. What she'd done back then was unforgivable.

The old mall photo on her monitor caught her eye—she and Dee making silly faces, two damaged girls who'd found each other. Back then, they'd both carried different kinds of pain. When they were together, it hurt less. The thought of leaving Dee after this would be worse than losing her mother's cold affection. Her friend made the world better just by existing. Allie might deserve jail, but Dee deserved none of this darkness. Her designer shoes—the ones she'd bought to catch a better life—stared accusingly from their box. She grabbed them and every other expensive thing she owned. Her fingers trembled as she set up the auction, but her product descriptions were perfect. She knew how to sell pretty lies. She'd learned from the best. By the time Dee's footsteps sounded on the stairs, Allie had sold five pieces above asking price. A few grand closer to freedom. But the charm bracelet seemed to pulse against her skin, a reminder that some things couldn't be bought or sold away.

"Hey, come up!" she called, pushing down the guilt. "I got good news!"

Dee bounded up the stairs, Kansas and Leander following shortly after.

Allison gestured toward the auction inventory, grinning. "I found a way to pay for a lawyer and support us—at least until we clear our name."

It took her friend a moment to register what Allie had meant. Her big eyes swept the room. "You're selling your stuff?"

"Yeah, call me a pawn star."

Dee rushed to her, snatching Allie in a huge bear hug.

Lee leaned on the doorway, his big body filling the frame. The poor guy watched the whole thing with no small amount of longing in his eyes. As the friends disentangled from their embrace, he cleared his throat. "I got a lot of projects coming in that I don't have the time for. If you two want to swing by the shop, we can split the profit."

His face lit up as Dee rushed in for the second bear hug. Allie, feeling a bit mischievous, threw herself into the mix. Watching the big guy stammer and blush was worth it.

Chapter Ten

NO FAIRY GODMOTHERS HERE

$\mathcal{D}$ee stood on the sidewalk, staring at a yellow door. When she'd called the office of Susan Glenda, she hadn't expected much. What did it matter if the attorney had advertisements all over town? That only meant she had money; not how successful she was. Dee had spent nearly an hour reading everything she could find about the lawyer, but most of it had to do with community involvement, attending the mayor's ball, organizing a luncheon for women in business, and holding a fundraiser for the historical society. But next to nothing about her skills as a lawyer. It didn't help that in the years Dee had lived in Sueños Del Mar, crime had never been one of her worries. Some of the residents creeped her out, of course, like the old man who was always walking. Even then, if she saw him coming, she'd cross the street or hide in Bertha or her house or wherever she happened to be and ... okay, yeah, that guy was super creepy. The cops should be looking his way instead of hers. She locked the front door most days, but didn't stress if it was accidentally forgotten. She could not imagine a criminal lawyer making enough money to even rent an office, let alone one in the center of town, in a recently refurbished building. Refurbished with help from the Historical Society, of course.

Maybe Susan Glenda did other things? Small claims or traffic court?

The website mentioned personal injury, traffic infractions, and misdemeanor-type offenses. Still, it didn't seem like enough to afford an office in this part of town. It was—

"Do you still want to go inside?" Allie asked, reaching out to gently release the twisted corner of Dee's cardigan from her fingers. "Because we don't have to. We can still wait to see if we are assigned a public defender."

Instead of answering directly, Dee said, "Where do you think she makes her money? Like, what *area* of law?"

"Um, I do not have any idea. Why does that matter?"

Dee tore her eyes from the yellow painted door long enough to see her friend gaping at her with confused concern. It seemed like that was the most frequent look she received these days. She knew she was letting the circumstances of recent events affect her more than she should. They were innocent, and this lawyer would help them prove it. Once they were able to put this behind them, things could go back to normal where she would be mildly anxious about a number of things, successfully hiding her worry behind a helpful and controlled façade. And then everyone would stop looking at her like she was on the edge of a breakdown.

"It's just, there's not a lot of crime around here and—"

Allie snorted, rolling her eyes, having moved on from confusion over Dee's random musing and onto mild exasperation. "Oh, please. There's plenty of crime everywhere. Just because you don't see it, doesn't mean it doesn't exist. I'm sure she keeps herself busy."

"But—"

"Let's go." Allie swept her arm through Dee's, dragging both of them through the door and into an inviting front waiting room.

Everything from the golden-brown hardwood flooring to the creamy wallpaper to the overstuffed couch set against the full-length front window was meant to welcome and put a client at ease. And if the interior decoration didn't work, the lavender essential oil steaming from a small humidifier should have. Unfortunately, there was nothing beyond someone declaring she and Allie innocent that would ease Dee. Also, she hated the smell of lavender.

Behind a sleek desk, a little person looked up from their keyboard, one eyebrow raised. "Appointment?" she asks, fingers poised to type in their information.

"Yes," Allie answered, stepping forward. "Allison Liddle and Dorseigh MacHale."

The receptionist nodded, her shiny black bob swishing with the movement. What was that like, Dee wondered absently, trying to get herself under control. She didn't want to be a nervous wreck when speaking to their lawyer for the first time. She wanted to project calm confidence and respectability. She wanted the lawyer to look at her and know there was no way she'd committed any crimes. The only way to do that was by distraction. She needed to think about literally anything else other than why they were here. Including the shiny swish of black hair. Dee's hair was too curly to ever swish. In fact, unless there was a strong wind, her hair pretty much stayed put.

The receptionist invited them to have a seat on the cushy couch while waiting for their appointment, which meant more time for Dee to spiral. Honestly, she was not going to make it through this entire ordeal.

"You got this," Allie murmured. "You run a business. You take care of your aunt and uncle. You are kind and giving, and once everyone gets their heads out of their asses, they will remember that."

She clung to those words while they waited, chanting them to herself until they were permitted into Susan Glenda's office. People would see. People would remember. There was nothing to worry about.

Susan Glenda looked just like her headshot. Shining blonde hair, deep rose-pink lips, apple-cheeked, and glowing. She stood to greet them as they entered her office, which was a little impersonal, if Dee was being honest. Where the foyer was warm and cozy, Susan Glenda's office was all modern lines with minimal decor. Black and white landscapes framed in thin black frames. A black iron floor lamp. Artfully arranged twigs in a gray vase. Even the client chairs were made for efficient space use and not comfort.

"Ladies." She was tall with either curves in all the right places or her pink Chanel suit was perfectly tailored to give the illusion of the perfect female form. "Please have a seat."

The chairs were straight backed and hard and uncomfortable

enough to force Dee to sit up straight. Somehow sitting with her shoulders squared, her back rigid, was what she needed to focus, to calm her nerves and behave like the responsible woman she knew herself to be.

"Now then," Susan Glenda smiled and asked, "how can I help you today?"

Dee took a deep breath, exhaled, and returned the smile. "I'm sure you've heard about our arrest."

"Oh, yes, it's all over town." She tsked, shaking her head. "What a lot of trouble for you two."

"Yes, well," Dee glanced at Allie, who gave her a nod. "I asked for a lawyer after the arrest, and I didn't receive one, and I still haven't been assigned any sort of defense. Neither has Allie. We assume once this goes to trial—"

"Oh," Ms. Glenda chuckled, interrupting. "That won't happen, dears. Don't you worry about that."

"Why won't it?" Allie asked, leaning forward just a little.

"Well, because it's absolutely ridiculous, isn't it?" The lawyer's smile turned slightly condescending as if she were speaking to children. "No one could actually believe you two committed these crimes."

"I mean, we think so. But the police—"

Again, Dee was cut off.

"The police." She rolled her eyes, shuffling some papers on her desk and straightening her keyboard. "We all know the police force is not exactly top notch."

Too bad neither were the lawyers, Dee thought, rubbing her suddenly sweaty palms on her dark blue slacks. Wherever this conversation was going, she did not feel like they were walking out of the office with representation.

"Now, let me tell you what I'll do for you, sort of like your very own fairy godmother."

Dee heard a muffled snort from Allie before she covered it with a cough. "I didn't know fairy godmothers wore Chanel."

The smile was demure. "Well, no one said I *was* a fairy godmother. Maybe I'm something other than that. Regardless, girls, I'll keep

Detective Doyle away from you until he's lost interest and he begins taking the investigation in a more natural direction."

"Lost interest," Dee repeated. At the same time, Allie asked, "What does a more natural direction mean?"

"Oh, you know, once they begin the real investigation. You two are a distraction, something to keep the town appeased until the actual culprit presents themself."

"What if they don't?" Dee asked, her voice curling up into a decibel it only reached in the most extreme circumstances, like being trapped in a cellar for hours and days, endlessly calling for her mother or father to let her out.

"Please. They will. You two girls have no reason to abduct children." She waved her perfectly manicured hand around as if brushing the absurd situation clean away. If only she could. If only she *was* a fairy godmother. "Now, you go out and about your business. Don't hide, but don't flaunt yourselves. Just be natural. The people will see the police were wrong, and then all of these nonsense charges will be dropped and you can put this all behind you."

A few minutes later, they were back out on the sidewalk, right where they started. No lawyer. No help.

"What now?" Dee asked, the way she felt sitting in the straight-backed chair dissolving as soon as her feet hit the concrete. At least Susan Glenda didn't charge them for her time.

"You know what? Forget her." Allie grabbed Dee, dragging her around the building to where they'd parked Bertha. "We don't need her. We'll just do this ourselves."

"Do what?" Dee asked, bewildered.

"We'll find whoever is doing this, and we'll start with Mrs. Thorne."

"What are we going to do?" Dee's voice crept up towards shrill, and she made an effort to wrangle it down to normal levels. "Stroll up and ask her what she's been up to lately? Why is she kidnapping children?"

"No. We're going to stake her out. Sit outside her house until we catch her in the act." Allie slid behind Bertha's wheel, her jaw set.

"What if she doesn't? What if she does nothing while the police suspect us? What if she waits until we are rotting in prison before she strikes again?"

Allie snorted, shaking her head. "I don't think so. She's got a reason to do this, and we're going to find out what it is."

"But, how? Doesn't she live in the hill behind a gate and a guard?"

Allison smirked. "Just leave that to me."

~

*I*f there was one thing he was good at, it was stripping in public.

True that in so many ways, he was sloppy, lazy, even careless sometimes. He could be known to take things for granted, to take people for granted. Which maybe could be forgiven once it was understood he was more than people, *other* than people, and sometimes he forgot what it meant to be simply human.

So, yes, he could be sloppy, lazy, careless, and all the other things he'd been called. But he was always fastidious when it came to stripping down in public.

Not that Highgate Park was public exactly. Yes, it was a public park, open to anyone, but few people ever visited it. It sat too close to the boundary and the boundary kept people away.

The boundary, however, did not have quite as much effect with the "more than people."

Which was inconvenient at the moment, seeing as how he was folding the last few bits of clothing into a tidy pile, standing stark-assed naked in the park, being watched by a damned white rabbit. Bunny? No, not bunny. Bunnies were rounded and fat. The thing twitching its nose at him from across the otherwise empty picnic area was long, lean, and a little wild. So, rabbit, then.

He'd smelled that rabbit before when it was in human form and he had a pretty good idea who it was, but neither of them would acknowledge it. They would continue to ignore each other in the street, even if they couldn't at the park.

Their eyes remained locked as he slid out of his human skin and into his other. Claws and teeth, fur roiling first under and then through, the tail. The rabbit watched his fall from two feet to four and then, like good little prey, took off into the surrounding trees, away from the boundary. He could hear it racing through the underbrush, his ears rotating to follow the noise. Smell it too, right in the roof of his mouth. Maybe one day he'd give chase, not that he'd ever be able to catch it. Male African lions weren't known for their hunting.

These days, after years of going through the change, it only twinged a little. Bones rearranging themselves tended to mess up pain receptors, he guessed, stretching, shaking out the tawny mane, running the rough tongue over his teeth. The first few times had been agonizing, his body learning to shift between forms without any guidance, without assurances that he wasn't dying, that he'd be okay. He'd trashed his house the first time, feral, frantic, and frenzied with fear. After that, he made sure to be outside. And, of course, these days he could control himself, could resist or give in even on the days when what he wanted, almost more than anything else, was to walk into the woods behind his house, shed his clothes, and take on the world in a different form. A different perspective. The problem was, there were no African lions in Northern California. If life were fair, he would change into a mountain lion. He could roam all over the upper state if that were the case, and no one would blink an eye as long as he wasn't feasting on people or livestock. But, no, that wasn't the fate afforded to him, and he was almost certain someone spotting a full grown male *Panthera leo* would blink, might call the incompetent cops. He could handle the cops, of course. If necessary. Even though as a general rule, he avoided confrontations as much as possible.

It was just easier that way.

If he had someone to talk to about whatever he was, he might feel better about the fact that he could shed his human form as easily as he could change a shirt. But there was no one. Or, to be exact, no one he trusted. He wasn't going to ask the rabbit. And since he couldn't remember parents or relations of any kind, that option wasn't available to him. In fact, he couldn't remember his life before a certain point, as if he sprang out of the clear blue. He dealt with that information the same way he dealt with everything—avoidance.

He started forward on thick paws, the strength in this body

flooding him with a confidence he did not feel anywhere else. In this body, he was a king.

The boundary was just on the other side of the clearing. He could see the trees start up again at the far edge, see how they thickened into an honest forest. Sometimes, if he concentrated enough, he could hear the rustling of small prey—squirrels and rodents, maybe an actual wild hare—but he couldn't smell them, had never seen them. The boundary kept them protected from him.

He advanced until his nose started to tingle with the warning to back away, just like the first time he discovered the boundary, like a predator had pissed along the town's edge. It hit him in the nose and made his fur stand on end. But he'd pushed on, determined to get as far away from his empty house with its small, square rooms and musty old smell as possible. He'd ignored the warning right up until his snout smacked the boundary.

The boundary was the second clue that things weren't quite right in Sueños Del Mar. He'd seen outsiders come through on the state highways. Had seen them leave, too. But, to his knowledge, not a single one of the residents ever left, ever seriously spoke of leaving. No vacations. No trips to the city. Those who were of the town stayed in the town. He didn't know if the boundary extended over the ocean, but he figured it did. Somewhere on the water, the illusion of freedom ended.

He paused. The boundary smelled different today, like sickly sweet rot. He pressed his flat nose against the slightly spongy surface, which was weird. Usually it was hard, usually it was enough to knock out a lion running full steam.

He growled, startling himself. He was always startled by the growl.

The boundary was getting thinner. Something in the animal part of his dual brain could sense it. Either the smell or the texture. Whatever was holding them in might not hold much longer.

If he'd been in his human form, he might have more thoughts about it. But in this form, he couldn't think much beyond the woods beyond, the freedom it would give him.

If the boundary failed, he could look for others like himself, look for answers.

With a grunt, he flopped down, rolling onto his back, four large paws sticking up in the air, stretching towards the patchy sunlight. If he found others like himself, he could do this whenever he wanted. He could lounge in the sun in cat form for as long as he wanted.

A snort and another roll and he was back on his feet, shaking his massive head. He wouldn't leave. Not now. Maybe not even if he could. Dee was here. Dee was in trouble. He would not leave her.

If he trusted himself, he'd tell her about this, about all the things he'd noticed in this town. But, no. She'd look at him like he was out of his mind. She might stop talking to him or showing up at his shop. She might not appreciate the way he showed up at the times she needed him. She might suspect he watched her.

She wouldn't be wrong, but she didn't need to know that.

No. He'd keep his observations and his secrets. He'd watch them, keep them safe, keep watching the boundary. Just like he'd been doing since the day he became fully aware that he was more than human and that there was something deeply wrong with Sueños Del Mar.

Chapter Eleven

HOUSE OF CARDS WITH A VIEW

Sueños Del Mar rose from beachfront to wealth in six sharp blocks, the terrain and home prices climbing in parallel. Allie's pulse raced as the Prius wound higher, each turn bringing them closer to the neighborhood she'd once called home and would love to forget.

"Remember how everyone in high school called this neighborhood Snob Knob?" Dee's hands held the steering wheel at the perfect ten and two taught in driving school.

The car smelled like old people, but the dinky electric car was quieter than Bertha's kerplunks, splutters, and rumbles. It also completely lacked any sort of personality other than the middle-class delusion that they could save the world through their personal choices.

The other advantage of the Prius—it didn't have Jills of All Trades on the door and Dee's cell phone number on the bumper sticker, so they were practically incognito.

"Remember in high school when everyone called this neighborhood 'snob knob'?"

Allie stared at the gates ahead, barely registering the question. The gate consisted of two boom barriers with a guard shack in between, but it felt as imposing as the iron spiked portcullis to the queen's castle in the game she loved. What she wouldn't give to be in her room playing that game rather than facing this part of her past. Well, not facing, but being adjacent enough that her throat felt like she'd swallowed an egg whole and it got stuck there—no a dozen whole eggs, shells and all, stopping up her throat. Her eyes burned, and slithering eels swam in her gut. Every instinct screamed to turn around, and she had to dig her fingernails into her palms to not tell her friend to do just that.

"Hey, you okay there?" Dee's gentle tone almost broke her.

Instead of crying, she girded herself with snark. "Not to be mean, but can we talk about how this car smells like arthritis cream and baby powder? How much must your aunt and uncle wear to make it permeate the upholstery?"

"I thought you were upset, but I should've known it was the reek of a nursing home that was getting to you." Her roommate chuckled, but the humor didn't quite reach her eyes.

Allie was grateful Dee went along with the joke.

The Prius reached the guard shack. Allie's stomach sank along with her plan to appeal to the elderly guard's sympathy. The old guard had given her a twenty-dollar bill when she'd moved out all her belongings from her mother's manse into a room in a boarding house. Fully emancipated, and disowned at the tender age of sixteen, she hadn't wanted to take his money, but she wanted someone, anyone to be kind to her.

Instead of the sweet, elderly gentleman, Jackson, a guy they went to high school with, stood in the guard shack. Jackson's hair was longer, and his beard was scruffier than in high school, but he still had the same bored look about him. His head was bent as he scrolled on his phone, ignoring them. He wasn't being intentionally rude. His job entailed letting people in when the badge key reader posted outside the shack didn't work.

With a heavy sigh, Dee rolled down her window. She put on her best midwestern girl-next-door smile and batted her eyelashes. "Hey, Jackson! I haven't seen you in forever!"

The guard scrambled to put his phone away. Not without flashing them a screen with a hentai image Allison would rather do without seeing. Ever. His gaze flicked to Dee and then to Allie. He smoothed a hand over his hair. "Hey. Didn't hear you pull up."

Dee smiled brighter. "Electric car. Can you buzz us in?"

He cleared his throat and straightened, finally remembering he was at work and had a modicum of authority, no doubt. "Do you have a badge?"

"Oh, we're here for a one-time job." Her roommate stiffened a little at the mention of a badge, but the dufus didn't seem to notice. Allie was proud that was Dee's only tell. Her friend rarely ever told falsehoods, with the exception of the white lies people told to make others feel comfortable.

Perhaps it was her Midwest earnest face that made Jackson nod and open the gate without checking the guest list. Perhaps he didn't give a flying hoot about his job. Either way, Allie let out her breath once they were through.

Dee glanced at Allie. "He can't get fired for this, right?"

Allie patted her shoulder, assuredly. "Nah. Nobody tries to get in here. The gates might as well be a ten-story wall surrounded by a moat."

Her roommate nodded, but doubt lingered in her eyes. Soon, Dee's jaw dropped as she drove the silent electric car through the neighborhood of sprawling mansions and manicured landscapes. Not a single pothole or crevice marked the private roads. It was as if the gated community were designed and built in a game instead of existing in real life.

"Allie, these houses are so..."

"Pretentious? Superfluous? Ostentatious? Never cleaned by the owners?"

She worked through the dueling disgust and apprehension to pretend she wasn't also intimidated. She no longer lived in the biggest mansion on the top of the hill. There were stipulations in the agreement with her mother she was breaking, too. Damn the stipulations. If they couldn't prove their innocence, she'd be getting exactly what those stipulations had once protected her against.

"I was going to say intimidating in their immaculate landscape and immensity of the homes. I thought some of our clients were rich."

"No, that's all an illusion. Banks own those homes and cars. Here, everything is owned by the people living in the houses." Including our town and the cops, she didn't add.

Dee shot Allison an incredulous look and waved at their surroundings in disbelief. "You really grew up here?"

"That's how the story goes, doesn't it?" Allie scowled at her own reply. *Funny that.* Having lost most of her childhood memories, she couldn't recall much before her teen years—especially before a certain event she'd rather forget but couldn't. Her therapist had said she'd lost her memory due to trauma—maybe she was right. She had to stop seeing her after her mother stopped paying for medical. Allison couldn't afford a therapist and get the heck out of this town. She'd see one once she cleared her name and found a way to finance her champagne dreams of decent mental health.

"Cryptic."

"That's me. Woman of mystery." Allie put on sunglasses. The thing was her life was a mystery. Occasionally, the rarest bits and pieces of her childhood came back to her in dreams. Some of it she was sure was entirely made up. In those dreams, her house was still immense, but the decor was about a hundred or so years out of date. She wore white pinafores and black Mary Janes. It was probably her brain confusing memories with the exorbitant amount of time she'd spent on fantasy games to avoid an antiseptic and loveless household.

She pointed to a spot up ahead. "Pull over there. Thorne's house is the one with the heart and animal shaped shrubs."

Dee wrinkled her nose at the sight. "Looks like Thorne's landscaper watched *Edward Scissorhands* too many times."

"My mother also has a landscaper who does topiary art. Others in the neighborhood started doing it. My mother once bragged at a party that she'd started the trend. Thorne overheard and disagreed. Her husband gave her the topiary art as an anniversary gift and paid top dollar for the best landscaper. There was a big feud between them about who started doing it first. The HOA almost banned new topiary design altogether."

Her roommate laughed, a hooting country guffaw. The lighthearted laugh after days of seriousness between them tickled her so much, she joined in. They giggled and snorted, almost forgetting why they were here. Almost. The niggling dread to clear their names and find out who harmed those poor kids lingered like a dark miasma threatening to suffocate their mirth.

They sobered as the garage door of Thorne's home opened. A red Cadillac backed out. Two heads were visible from the vehicle's rear window.

"Duck!" Dee squeaked.

They slid down in their respective seats, heartbeat racing in Allie's chest. It was during the middle of the day, but Thorne was old. Maybe she didn't even notice the Prius?

After she could no longer hear the Caddy's engine, Allie sat up and turned to Dee. "They left the garage door open. Let's go check it out."

All the color faded from her roommate's normally rosy cheeks. "I thought we were going to just stake out her house. That sounds risky. What if we're caught on surveillance cameras?"

"Hello? Gated community. No one is stealing from anyone else here. The cameras are on the plebes outside this little piece of Heaven." She waved her hand dismissively, unbuckling with the other. "Besides, what if she has the kids in there? We'll be their saviors."

Dee pursed her lips and eyed the open garage. "Let's take some cleaning gear with us, so it looks like we're here for a job."

Allie hooted and fist pumped. "Yeah! That's what I'm talking about."

Crossing the street, with the sprawling manse on the hill that she used to call home seemingly watching her imperiously above, she lost some of her initial nerve. Actually, she had no clue if anyone had cameras. She hoped they'd find evidence so that it wouldn't matter. Besides, she'd watched enough true crime shows to know that it wasn't breaking and entering if the door was unlocked.

"Just a quick snoop around the garage," Dee whispered as if reassuring herself, not talking to Allison.

She brushed a stray lock of blonde hair out of her face. "Sure."

"What if there are kids in the house? They wouldn't be in the garage."

Allie glanced at her roommate. Dee gnawed her lip, but there was anger in her blue gaze. She swallowed her own building fear and thought about the poor kid she'd found half dead, tossed like trash between her bins. "I guess we can see if the door is unlocked and take a quick look."

Determination set on her pretty face. "Just a quick sweep so our conscience is clear."

"Sure."

Two bushes shaped like hearts upon stands guarded the driveway. Rose bushes climbed trellises that covered a good majority of the outside of the house. Every single rose was the deep red of blood, causing a frisson to skitter across Allie's shoulders. What if Thorne was up to some really horrible things, and they were walking right into it? What if they found an actual dead body? At what cost would clearing her name come?

Throwing her shoulders back, Allie reminded herself that anything she saw wouldn't be as bad as prison. A piece of her wanted to stomp and cry at the unfairness of this. Between her burgeoning fanbase for her live streams and the millionaire dating app—which she had totally used doctored screenshots of her old trust fund to get on the app in the first place—she had her out. Leaving this damned town and traveling abroad had been just within her grasp. Then, this happened. She went from escaping this small-town prison to the possibility of actual prison. She and Dee would clear their names. They had to.

The garage was nothing out of the ordinary. Bins on shelves only contained holiday decorations that she was sure Thorne paid people to put up and take down each season. Mr. Thorne's Bentley didn't have anything in the glove compartment or the trunk either.

Allie and Dee put on hair caps and gloves they used for particularly messy odd jobs. She tried the door with a gloved hand. The knob turned, and the door swung open, revealing a mudroom that didn't have a speck of dirt. The granite floor shone with a fresh wax job.

"Let's put on footies, too," Dee wisely suggested.

From the mudroom they entered the main great room of the house. The place smelled so strongly of roses that Allie almost gagged. She normally enjoyed the scent, but it was too much. She pulled a bandana out of her case and wrapped it around her face, tying it behind her head. Dee did the same.

The house had minimalist furniture in shades of white, red, and black. Red roses filled vases on every available surface. The art had a strange, Dali-esque quality to it. Each piece seemed like a window into a bizarre fantasy world.

One portrait above the mantel stood out from the rest—Thorne, much younger, dressed in Nineteenth Century, European regalia, complete with a crown and scepter. She sat in a high back chair that resembled a throne. Next to the chair and slightly behind, Mr. Thorne stood also dressed as finely but wore no crown, as if he were consort, not king. The picture was ostentatious, but captivating. As if Thorne and her husband really were nobility.

What troubled Allie is that she had a similar painting of her family in her home. They were all dressed in period pieces, not quite royalty, but nobility/ Or, at the very least, London bourgeois of the Victorian Era. In the painting, she'd worn a white pinafore just like in her dreams. She had no memory of posing for the family portrait—again, not that she remembered much of her childhood. Perhaps looking at the painting influenced the dreams.

"Should we split up?" Dee's voice took her out of her head, breaking the spell the art had on her.

"Why are you whispering?"

"I don't know. What if they have live-in staff?"

Allie snorted. "Thorne is particular with her things and fires anyone who doesn't meet her standards. She doesn't keep anyone for more than a week, so her husband hired a service to come clean and maintain the property. The service rotates whoever comes so they only have to tolerate her abuse once a month."

Dee cocked her head to one side. "How do you know this?"

"If you think small town gossip is bad, try a gated community."

She clucked her tongue disapprovingly. "You'd think they'd have better things to do with their time with all the money they have."

"People are people no matter how much they have, Dee. How about I take upstairs, and you take down here? Then we meet up and do the basement together?"

"It's a California home built after the 1960s. There is no basement."

"They have them on Snob Knob, Dee."

Her eyebrows shot up, and then she shrugged. "All right. Let's just do a quick sweep and get out of this place. Meet here in ten minutes?"

"Yeah. Keep your cell close, in case we need to text each other."

Upstairs, she went through every room. Eyes on the surfaces and hands opening closets. She ignored the pull to stare at art. There was no time.

Finally, in Thorne's room, in a dresser drawer, she found a key. It was an old-fashioned key like one you'd see in an antique shop. She pocketed it. If there was anything or *anyone* in the basement, she bet this key would unlock it.

~

*R*euben sat in the tree in cat form, watching Allie go from room to room. *Stupid, stupid, stupid* repeated in his head to the beat to his rapid pulse. *Why would they go inside the Thornes' house? Was she stealing?* He shook out his body and then stretched languidly.

No, Allison would rob anyone blind if it meant getting away from this town, but Dee wouldn't be up to no good.

He'd almost believed they were here on a job, but they'd ducked when Thorne had passed.

The tree shook. *What the...*

A lion clambered up the trunk.

Every hackle in his body rose. He arched his spine, threw his ears back and hissed.

The lion froze and ... cringed? Part of him wanted to yowl in victory, but the human side asked, what kind of lion cringed at a house cat?

Reuben pushed through his feline fight or flight response and used his human logic. There are no wild lions in Sueños Del Mar, only a big idiot that shifted into one. He used the telepathy of shape shifters.

Sorry. Instinct.

Scared the hell out of me. I thought you were a cat-cat and would scratch my eyes out.

Reuben would have laughed if he were in human form. The ostensible king of the jungle afraid of a tomcat was too rich. The lion finished the climb and settled into a two-branch crook.

Are they in there?

Yeah.

We got to get them out. The Thornes are at the gate.

Reuben scurried down the tree to his clothes piled in a bush nearby. He batted at the phone, then gave up and used his teeth to pull it out of his jeans pocket. It took him a moment to realize he couldn't unlock the screen let alone make a phone call in this form. It was a big risk shifting here on Snob Knob, but he'd transformed in worse places with less worthy risks. Besides, if he didn't get Allison out of there, she'd be in more trouble than she already was—Thorne had the similar stink of foul magic that was on the kids.

The transition from beast to man and man to beast was always a hazy affair. Like a fever dream and waking up. He didn't feel a thing, and it took a few moments for him to remember who he was and what he'd been doing. Dazedly, he put the phone in front of his face.

"Call Allie," he commanded the phone. He'd explain to her how he got her number later. She would be pissed but alive.

The call went to voicemail. Of course, it did. She probably had it on silent while she broke and entered the Thornes.

He blinked a few times, his mind and vision adjusting to being human. Since her contact was up, he pressed the little icon that would take him to the messenger feature on his phone. He typed, "Get out." After hiding the phone again, he shifted into the cat form. That also took several moments to adjust to. When he regained his feline senses, Reuben spoke telepathically to Leander.

Head the Thornes off to give the girls time to get the heck out of here.

On it.

The lion jumped from the tree, loping down the street at a pace that would do a pride hunting gazelles justice. Well, if Lee was going to brave heading Thorne off, Reuben would stay and watch out for the ladies from above. He ran over to the tree, pounced on the trunk, and scurried up. Movement caught Reuben's attention below—Allie and Dee ran out the garage, gear in tow.

Yes! She'd received the message and listened for a change.

"I don't know who sent it," Allie whisper-shouted loud enough for his extra-feline hearing, "but I'm not kicking a gift horse in the mouth."

To the south, he saw Thornes' car heading up the hill and fast. He also saw a lion now running right straight for the vehicle at a pace usually saved for chasing antelopes.

Thorne must've seen the lion and hit the brakes. The vehicle careened. The lion adjusted his course, running over the hood onto the roof. The weight of the massive beast dented the hood and roof. Reuben couldn't see them, but he bet the Thornes were cowering and pissing their pants. He would laugh, but he wasn't in human form, and this was no time to laugh.

Relief sprang in his chest light and airy as the Prius took off in the opposite direction of the Thornes' seized vehicle.

Chapter Twelve

DUNGEONS AND PURPLE DRAGONS

I know she has it. I have felt it thrice now whenever she is nearby. I do not know how it came to be in her hands nor how long she has had it, but I know it is her. This girl, she knows nothing about this world I have created, but she is still sensitive to the magic. I know she feels the pull of the power item.

My key.

My *missing* key.

I had thought to walk up to her and take it, but she is never alone, and too much magic gathered in one place makes my words of suggestion weaker. Weaker, at least, than when I use them on someone with much, *much* less magic.

And so I find myself in some place I do not care to be.

When I willed this place into being, there was a window, a pocket of time, when I was recovering, before I understood what it would truly take to make this town continue to exist. During that time, the people who were here before, assimilated with my people. Once I realized what had happened, it was too late to expel them, too much magic required. And, so they stayed inside my world, but outside my full control. Thus, I avoid them as much as I am able.

Which is why, as I walked into the police station full of the outsiders, I asked to speak to Doyle and only to Doyle. He remained one of the few officers under my control. Tedious, to be sure. But, while I may have brought my people here, I do not control every aspect of their lives. I cannot force them to join the law enforcement team.

"Sir." He holds a chair for me at his small desk, a look of confusion on his face. That's all right, though. I'm used to that look. "What can I do for you today?"

"I need you to do something for me, my boy." I release the smallest wisp of magic. Green, a little shimmery, pleasantly scented. It's the magic that coaxes, that conjoles, that persuades.

The intelligence in his eyes dims, replaced by a slightly glazed look. He nods.

I tell him about the girl. Her name. He knows her name, of course, in his normal state of mind, but not here. Not now. I tell him what she looks like, what she drives. I tell him where she is—riding with her roommate in the aunt's car. I tell him where she's going, but not why she's there. The girls are on their own chase. Looking for clues where they may or may not exist. But, that isn't relevant to what I want.

I tell him to bring her to the station, to get the item of power from her, and to return it to me.

He says, "Yes, sir," like a perfect drone, completely under my thrall.

"I will wait for you," I say. Standing. I will not wait here, in this station. I will take a walk, nod to my people, and watch for him to return with the girl. And then I will walk back to his desk and have my item of power.

⁓

*D*ee's heart sped faster than the Prius as they accelerated through the neighborhood, hands clutched on the steering wheel with white-knuckled intensity. Since she'd never driven through Snob Knob, taking random corners was probably not the best escape plan, but her screaming blood did not care where they went. Only that they went far away.

"Dee," Allie shouted, bracing herself on the dashboard as the Prius screeched around a curve. "What are you doing? Slow down!"

She was almost certain it wasn't the first time Allie had shouted it in the few minutes since they'd left the Thornes' house. Unfortunately, her brain seemed to be detached from her body, because she couldn't seem to let off the pedal.

Finally, after narrowly missing a parked car, she registered Allie's shriek about a cat, managing to focus on a distant feline trotting across the street at least a half block away. She eased off the acceleration, applying gentle pressure to the brake and finally rolling to a stop along a grassy curb.

"I'm sorry," she breathed, turning toward her friend. "Maybe I shouldn't be the getaway driver anymore."

Allie exhaled a soft, slightly manic giggle. "It's a good thing there aren't any cliffs for you to drive off."

Dee's head fell forward, bouncing off the steering wheel. "I would have, too. I didn't even see where I was going. Please never tell my aunt about this."

"I feel like if the cops observed our escape, they would write us off the suspect list."

"Why? Because I clearly cannot keep my head in the most minor of stressful situations?"

Allie giggled again, a little less manically this time. "There's not a cool bone in your body."

She took a few deep breaths before sitting back up, eyeing the houses looming on either side of the street, shadows beginning to stretch in the early evening. Finally, once her blood pressure returned to normal, she put the car back into gear and eased away from the curb.

"What should we do now?"

"I don't know," Allie sighed. She held an ancient-looking key in the palm of her hand. "I found this. In their bedroom."

Dee started reaching for it, momentarily distracted by the street-lights flickering on, a stray beam of light catching on the silver shoe charm of Allie's bracelet. She blinked, giving herself a shake. "What do you think it opens?" The key was weighty, heavier than any key she'd held before, like it was pure iron, and slightly rusty. "A treasure chest?"

"Or," Allie snatched it back, "a door where they keep children. I'm thinking something in an unfinished basement type of setting, behind a brick wall, with shackles and straw on the floor."

"Like a dungeon?"

Allie snapped her fingers. "Exactly."

"I found a locked door," Dee revealed. "In the kitchen. And I thought that was pretty weird, right? Why would they have a locked door when it's just the two of them living there? That makes no sense."

Allie cursed. "We have to go back."

"I figured you were going to say that."

"Too bad we can't go right now. Too bad Jackson is never going to fall for our story again."

"We could try to come back on foot?"

Allie shot the idea down as soon as it was out of Dee's mouth. Irksome. She both hated being contradicted and believed everything she said was wrong. Arguments were hell, which was why she mostly avoided being in them.

According to Allie and backed up by Dee's very recent memory of driving to the neighborhood, there weren't any inconspicuous pull-offs. It would be better to drive home, park the Prius, and hoof it all the way back. Which, fine, they could do that. It would probably take them about forty-five minutes. But then there was the issue of casually walking around the only gated neighborhood in town well after dark without any excuse as to why they were there.

Dee drove aimlessly while they contemplated where to go next. The need to get back inside the house, to properly explore what was behind the locked door and whatever else was hidden in the Thornes' house sat on Dee's shoulders like an anxious little imp, urging her to go now, to get it over with now, to clear their names now, now, *now*.

After twenty minutes of driving down one street and then the next, circling everywhere except for the street the Thornes lived on, Allie sighed, saying, "We're going to have to do this now."

Dee's phone buzzed with a conveniently incoming text. She read the message and then asked, "Do you ever wonder if someone is listening to us?"

She flipped the screen towards Allie, who cursed again at the message Leander sent, letting them know Mrs. Thorne was bringing her car to him immediately, that he wouldn't be around later if she needed him because it sounded like a job they expected him to complete while they waited.

"Did he know? Did you tell him what we were doing?"

"Absolutely not," Dee said vehemently, red curls bouncing as she shook her head. She wasn't about to drag him into her problems more than he was already in them. Besides that, he would have tried to talk her out of their plan, as any sane person would. They cleaned up messy houses and made minor repairs. They weren't detectives. Dee didn't even read mystery novels and was terrible at escape rooms. She knew this entire scheme was likely pointless, but it was better than hiding in their house waiting for another child to go missing. There was *no way* she let Leander know what they were doing.

"Do you have plans with him later?" Allie asked slyly. "Finally?"

"What's that mean? What does finally mean?" Dee squeaked, slamming her foot on the brakes.

Allie shrugged, failing to hide a smirk. She pointed to a particularly shady stretch of street, indicating they should pull back over, explaining how they should walk, that it would be less conspicuous than continuing to drive through the neighborhood in the car they'd just used to speed away from what some might consider a breaking-and-entering type of situation.

"Too bad," she whispered, as they walked away from the Prius, "that we really will have to break in this time."

"Maybe they left the garage door open?" Dee chewed a thumbnail, trying not to think about the growing darkness or if anyone watched them from the massive windows of the surrounding houses. "What do you think happened to them? Maybe they crashed their car trying to speed away with another kid."

"What I want to know," Allie mused, fingering the charms on her bracelet, "is who freaking texted us to get out."

"Can't you just call the number?"

"I did," Allie replied, shrugging. "Voicemail not set up. I sent a text, too, but nothing yet."

They walked in silence on a wide, even sidewalk. Dee bet if the neighborhood had any kids, they'd never crashed their bikes on broken concrete. Never skinned a knee after flying off their seat or cracked their elbow hard enough to take their breath away. She bet all the parents could afford brand new helmets and never had to pick gravel out of bloody shins. Her legs were a map of childhood injuries. Of childhood memories. And even though most days she tried to actively suppress those memories before they led to even harder and more painful ones, she was glad they existed. They were a reminder that her parents and her life had existed before this town.

Allie groaned as they rounded a curve that led down a gentle decline, dead-ending into the Thornes' street. Their house sat midway up the block, garage doors down, all lights off, save for the two solar coach lanterns on either side of the garage doors.

"Call Lee," Allie said, stopping on the decline in the shadow of an ancient tree.

"Uh, okay. Why?"

"Confirm the Thornes are still with him. We're going to need all the time we can get trying to get back inside."

"Oh. All right."

He answered on the fifth ring with a breathless, "Yeah? I mean, hey. What's up?" She could hear a door slam and something metal crashing to the ground.

"What are you doing? Did you just walk into a closet?" She could picture the exact closet, too. It was barely deep enough to hold anything, so he'd installed a pegboard for some of his more expensive tools.

"What?" There was a thump and then a curse. "Sorry. Fuck. I mean, sorry."

She was tempted to laugh at him, except bumbling wasn't like Leander, and she was suddenly worried something was wrong.

"Sorry. I just walked in the door. The Thornes were waiting for me, and you know how she is. What's going on? Did you get my message?"

"Yeah, actually, that's why I'm calling. Are you at home or your shop?"

"House. I'm—did you need something?"

"No. I didn't mean to bother you. Um, so the Thornes are still there?"

He took a deep breath, and she could picture him scrubbing at his face. "Yeah. I've got at least an hour of work. Maybe more. They're paying me to get it done tonight, so I'm getting it done tonight."

"What happened?" she asked, ignoring a look of impatience from Allie.

After a hesitation, he said, "You won't even believe me. I'll fill you in later, okay?"

"Sure. Or whatever. You don't have to. It's no big deal."

"Hang up," Allied hissed.

"No, it's—"

"Okay, I have to go. Talk to you later." She ended the call, placing her phone on silent. "They're there. Sounds like they beat him home from wherever he was. He says at least an hour."

"Well, great, since we'll need all of it to figure out how to get inside."

"I left a bathroom window open." Dee slid her phone into a back pocket, ignoring Allie staring at her agog. "That's what I was doing when you called for us to run. I figured it might come in handy in case we needed to get back in. There's no screen, so I figured—Ooof."

Allie slammed into her, wrapping her up in a hug sort of like what she imagined a death grip would be like.

"Holy shit, that's amazing. I take back what I said about you not being cut out for crime. You totally are."

Dee allowed the contact for longer than she normally would. Dimly, she recognized that she was wound so tightly, she was sure to snap at some point in the very near future. But it wasn't right at that moment, so she disentangled herself, stepping away. "We don't have much time."

Even in the darkness, she saw Allie roll her eyes. "Yeah, yeah. Affection bad, I know. C'mon. Let's go explore locked doors in a house with strange art."

"Strange art?"

"Never mind. Let's go."

The window, at the back of the house, was small, but not too small for Allie and not so high that she couldn't pull herself in without issue. Thirty seconds later, a small beam of light bounced across the room and to the sliding door that opened into a room that was probably a family room, but that the Thornes had transformed into a strange art gallery, with an inappropriately poised statue of...

"Is that Mrs. Thorne?" Dee gasped, choking.

"I'm not looking. You can't make me." Allie put her hands to either side of her eyes, determinedly moving forward, holding the flashlight of the phone outward and down. "Where is the door?"

"Kitchen. There's a pantry larger than our dining room, and it's at the back."

"A locked door in a pantry? That is intriguing. Why were you in the pantry?" Allie expertly guided her through the maze of lower-level rooms all while keeping her eyes glued to the floor, like the artwork might dazzle her if she made eye contact.

"Well, I started in the kitchen, you know? And it was pretty boring, actually, because I don't think they ever cook anything or eat here because the cabinets are literally bare, so I found the pantry, which is also bare and then..." They'd reached the pantry and pushed the door open into a large room with mostly empty shelves.

"Wow." The locked door was everything Allie was looking for, as far as Dee could tell. It was heavy, old, and looked like it would only open via a rusty iron key.

Allie strode confidently, the key in hand, phone in the other, only to be disappointed almost immediately. The doorknob was modern and used a modern key.

"Now what?" Dee asked, wringing her fingers. Just a little.

"Now we find the key that fits this lock. I think." Allie pocketed the old key. "Yeah, I'm pretty sure I saw something upstairs in their room." And then she bolted out the door, leaving Dee fumbling in the dark until she fished out her own phone and turned on the flashlight app.

Around her, the house remained completely silent save for the distant thumping of Allie's feet. She was tempted to send Leander a message asking how things were going, but they were not allies in this. He couldn't know what they were doing, and she'd never randomly messaged him just because. Especially after calling him. That wasn't the sort of relationship they had. She'd like to have it, though. Maybe. But she'd never pursue it, and he obviously didn't think about her like that or else he would have started something, right?

Stop, she chided herself. *There are more important things to think about right now.* Like the fact they had crawled through their landlady's bathroom window and were currently rummaging through her house, looking for evidence that she was kidnapping children. That was more important than ... whatever happened (Or not!) between her and some guy.

"Hey, I got another key." Allie slipped back into the pantry.

"How the hell did you even find that?" She crowded her roommate as she watched the key turn in the lock, the door clicking open.

Allie shrugged and said breathlessly, "I have a knack." She looked over her shoulder at Dee. "You ready?"

Absolutely not. She would probably never be ready.

She nodded and Allie swung the door wide, revealing steps down into who knew what.

～

"*I*s that a dragon?" Was Dee's first question once Allie located and flipped on a dim ceiling light. Which, considering the scene before them, was really the last thing that should have caught her attention.

"No. Not a dragon. A jabberwocky," Allie stated confidently from where they both stood rooted at the bottom of the steps. "And it appears to be fornicating with Mrs. Thorne."

"A what-a-wocky?"

"Jabberwocky. It's a..." Allie paused. "I'm not actually sure what it is."

"Do you think she considers Mr. Thorne to be her purple jabberwocky?" Dee's brain, once again, had put her on autopilot. Words could form, they could come out of her mouth, but she had no idea what she was looking at, what this room *was*.

"I refuse to answer that, because that means I have to think about it."

"What is this place?" Dee took one step backward onto a step.

Allie took one forward into the room. "I think we found their sex dungeon." She pointed to the black rack along one wall from which hung a variety of harnesses, straps, a couple whips, and other things Dee's autopilot brain could not identify.

"Are those dildoes?" She squeaked, pointing at a glass cabinet, not too dissimilar to one her aunt had. Only Aunt Sal displayed tea sets and not synthetic penises in a dazzling amount of sizes.

The room wasn't huge and they couldn't see any other doors or places to hide children. There certainly wasn't anyone hanging from the swing that dangled from the ceiling or the benches or the cross or...

"We need to go. *I* need to go."

"Yeah," Allie agreed. "Let's get out of here."

They turned off the light and ran back up the stairs, through the pantry, Allie tossing the key somewhere on the way back to the window. They shimmied through—Allie easier than Dee—shutting it behind them and trying to casually walk back to the car. Dee had to chant to herself to walk, walk, *walk*, do not run. She highly doubted anyone jogged in this neighborhood, especially not in jeans and a cheap hooded sweatshirt.

They were almost to the car. They were going to make it. Of course they were. No one knew they were here or what they were doing. It was all so easy, even if they didn't find concrete evidence. There was the old key and some amount of deviance, even if it seemed to be only for the enjoyment (choke) of a married couple. They would just need to figure out what the iron key went to and –

"Hello, ladies," came a male voice from the direction of the Prius.

They stopped as a form stepped away from the car and a high-beam flashlight clicked on in their faces.

"Odd area for a walk for two people who don't live here."

"Detective Doyle," Allie purred. "I have friends in the area."

"Hmmm." The detective waved the flashlight toward another car parked directly behind the Prius. "Why don't the three of us take a little ride together."

"Why?" Dee squeaked. "We aren't doing anything wrong."

Because that was true. They were *walking*. If he'd found them in the sex dungeon, she probably wouldn't have been able to get the words out, because she wouldn't have believed them herself. Obviously, they shouldn't have been in the Thornes' house, but *walking*?

"Well, I'm thinking maybe you are."

He was so nonchalant, standing there, shining the ferocious beam of the flashlight in their eyes, suggesting they go with him back to jail. It hit her all at once that she hated him. How dare he? There was an actual person out there harming children, but he wouldn't find them because he was too busy bothering them.

"I'll drive us behind you," she said, squaring her shoulders. "And call our lawyer on the way there."

She couldn't see his face, due to the blinding light in hers, but she felt him watching them. Long seconds dripped by without a sound from the three of them. Somewhere nearby, a door opened, the noise of a loud family discussing an upcoming game filled the air, softening the tension a small amount, but not enough for Doyle to reply.

"Okay, great." Dee pulled out her keys. "See you there. Let's go, Allie."

"Who are you?" Allie whispered, following behind her.

~

The police station had not changed over the last week. Like their first trip, they were separated and questioned. Only, this time, Dee didn't speak. She let them know she wanted her lawyer and wouldn't speak without her. The Sueños Del Mar police department did not like being told to wait and so they kept asking her why she was in Snob Knob, who she was visiting, and for how long. She thought about sharing their theory on the Thornes, but didn't want to incriminate herself any more than she already had the first time through.

In the end, Susan was not answering her phone, Dee wasn't talking, and Detective Doyle decided to hold them overnight on trespassing, which Dee was nearly certain wasn't legal. She'd certainly have something to say to Susan Glenda, as soon as she started answering her phone.

Chapter Thirteen

COPS AND ROBBERS

*D*etective Doyle loomed across the Formica table, turning her charm bracelet over in his hands with unsettling focus. They'd already tried to break Dee— her roommate had returned from questioning tight-lipped and ashen, a curt head shake confirming Susan Glenda hadn't shown.

This had to be illegal. Even basic crime shows taught her about Miranda rights, about lawyers. But nothing in Sueños Del Mar worked quite like it should. She thought money had greased the wheels of her release years earlier, but perhaps it was not just that. Maybe everything was corrupted? Like black mold had gotten into everyone's brains and made them all a little paranoid and delusional.

The metallic clink of charms filled the silence as Doyle examined each one like a mystic reading runes. All present except the rabbit charm now hidden in her mouth, its familiar weight pressing against her tongue. Let them search through whatever came next—she wouldn't surrender this one piece of real magic, even if it meant tasting platinum and guilt for days to come. The charm was too unique, too easily connected to the comatose boy they'd found.

"Fond of jewelry?" The words slipped out before she could stop them.

Doyle's eyes snapped up, that careful mask of a bumbling detective falling away. He dangled the bracelet between them like bait. "You're missing one—a peculiar magnifying glass charm."

Ice slid down her spine. A magnifying glass? Everyone saw something different in that charm, but he shouldn't have noticed its absence at all. Her pulse roared in her ears as she fought to keep her expression neutral.

"I'm broke," she managed, the charm burning against her tongue. "Your witch hunt cost me everything. I'd sell my soul to keep the lights on."

His hairy knuckles gleamed white as he set the bracelet down with deliberate care. "Speaking of witch hunts—why visit the old neighborhood? The one your mother banished you from?"

Terror froze her blood. No one knew about that—her mother had buried those secrets under money and influence.

"The guard shack keeps interesting lists." He pulled a clipboard from his bag, eyes glinting with predatory intelligence. "Your name features prominently. We both know why."

The room tilted sideways as he produced a laptop. "Quite the history, Allison. Petty theft. Vandalism. Standard teenage rebellion..." His mustache twitched with dark amusement. "Until it wasn't."

She stared at that strip of hair above his lip, letting the present fade. Better to drift than remember that day. Better to float than face what she'd really done, what she'd really been running from all this time.

Run, run, run! Her mind screamed as her feet scrambled up the spiral stone staircase. Her hands reached out in the dark for balance, scraping the stone walls. She had no plan except escaping the demon behind her.

"You stole my watch, you fucking bitch!" Echoed up the stairwell.

She reached the top. A covered, open-air overpass connected the dorms to the main campus building and faculty offices. If she could get across, someone from the staff would see her and she could get help. Out of immediate danger, she'd find a way to spin this all on him. If she didn't, her mother would cover it up. He'd get kicked out of the school, and she wouldn't worry about a thing.

Present and past collided as Doyle's voice cut through the memory. "The school incident doesn't appear in official records. Funny how money can make certain things." He paused for obvious dramatic effect. "Disappear."

Nevertheless, her pulse thundered in her throat. The charm pressed against her tongue like a secret trying to choke her.

"But the guard's list tells an interesting story." He tapped the clipboard. "Banned at sixteen. No visitors, no contact. Your own mother paid to make you vanish." He leaned forward, his cologne carrying a whiff of something older, earthier. "What did you really do, Allison?"

Before her foot landed on the wooden overpass, a hand grabbed her hoodie. Allison was airborne, arms and legs pinwheeling.

"Give it back!" Spittle flew from his mouth. His normally pale skin turned the color of a ripe eggplant. His light blue eyes bulged from their sockets.

"The missing children." Doyle's voice dragged her back. "They're found in a coma." His eyes fixed on where the rabbit charm should be. "Reminds me of another case. A boy in a boarding school, found similarly. Sprawled below an overpass."

She couldn't have heard him right. That case was buried, vanished, forgotten like she was supposed to be.

"Tell me, Miss Liddle." He pulled an evidence bag from his messenger bag. Inside, a pocket watch gleamed with familiar malice. "Ever seen this before?"

The room spun.

"Allison?"

Allie blinked and shook her head. A shiver ran through her, and she involuntarily rubbed her arms in response. She hadn't thought about that day since high school. She'd carefully, thoroughly avoided thinking about it. The further she got away from this town, the further she'd be from the damned nightmare of her past. Rallying, she eyed the detective as if he were an insignificant worm. "Shoplifting and petty theft were never proven. Jealous clerks made false accusations and ruined my life. Even if I was a thief, that doesn't mean I'd hurt little kids."

"Was it an accident or are mummy's pockets that deep?"

She looked Doyle in the eye. "A feral stray attacked my boyfriend when we were on a walk. He lost his balance." She'd said the line so many times, it was like second nature to respond. Good thing the detective couldn't sense how her stomach knotted with the half-truth. However, he was good.

"He had scratch marks on him. Some were from a cat ... others that didn't match a cat."

"I tried grabbing him. My nails were long."

"You had defensive wounds."

The prosecuting attorney tried to give her that out, too. She'd wanted to take the plea bargain. However, she stuck to the story her mother's attorney gave her.

"He tried to grab me for purchase. It happened fast and was years ago. Do you know what it's like to be sixteen and lose your first love, Detective?"

"Love? His family said a valuable family heirloom was missing from his belongings, and they were sure he wouldn't have given it to—" He cleared his throat. "I'm sorry. Their words, not mine. The campus slut."

That one stung. She hadn't slept with anyone but the jerk, but boys lied about sleeping with pretty girls. She'd fed into the lie. It made her more popular without having to actually do anything. "Again, stealing and having sex with random as a teenager doesn't make me a kidnapper or someone who harms little kids."

"It doesn't make you look innocent either." Doyle switched tactics. "Give me something to help you out."

Her gaze went directly to the key. She let it linger there.

The detective noticed and picked it up. "What does this unlock?"

She shrugged and pursed her lips. "Can't say. I found it in my backyard."

A gleam shone in the detective's eyes as he regarded the key. Without looking at her, he asked. "The same backyard where the boy was found?"

Technically, she found him in the alley between her house and the neighbor's fence, but potato potato. Allie nodded and then furrowed her brow.

Doyle's gaze snapped from the key to her face. "Are you remembering something?"

"It's just—well—Thorne stopped by that day, or was it the next? It might be hers. She has peculiar ... predilections."

She watched the wheels turn as he considered her words, until he finally spoke. "Care to elaborate?"

"Well, I'm not one hundred percent sure, but I heard that Thorne's got some weird stuff going on in her basement. Also, did you know that all the victims' families are tenants of hers?"

The detective stared at her unyieldingly.

Allie didn't buckle under the weight of his stare, but she was sure glad Dee wasn't there. Her roommate finally showed some gumption, but Dorseigh usually fawned at the very idea of confrontation with authority.

The door to the interrogation room swung open. A harried woman in her mid-thirties burst in. "Another kid has been found!"

The detective pocketed the key and rushed to the door.

"Hey! Doesn't that mean I can go?"

Doyle gestured to someone beyond the door. "See to someone processing their release, would you?"

"It's my job as their lawyer to free them." Glenda Susan popped her head in. "Ah, yes, yes it does. It also means you two can't be the abductors."

∼

For years he'd watched Allison, first seeing her on that overpass—not just a girl in trouble, but something more. A connection thrummed between them, inexplicable as his ability to shapeshift, forbidden as the border he'd discovered.

Something intangible yet very real connected him to her, whether she knew it or not. Her brilliance, her beauty—they were just facets of whatever power drew him to her like a moth to a flame.

The familiar tug seized his gut. *No. Not now.* Two steps up, an invisible force yanked him back. Cotton filled his head as his vision blurred. He screamed inside his locked jaw, knowing what came next, knowing he was powerless to stop it.

Reality blurred past, like a movie on fast-forward. When it settled, he stood in the park, human form betraying him.

"Put these on, cat." The witch thrust sweats and a hoodie at his chest.

His silent rage burned useless in his throat as his body obeyed. Bitter hatred rose—not just for her control, but for the memories she'd steal from him until next time.

"That one." She pointed to a boy pedaling fast on his bike.

His body moved with feline grace between the trees. One stick, one precise movement—the bike went down. He snatched the stunned boy faster than human eyes could track, guilt churning as the child's head lolled against his shoulder.

T'he witch's words crawled over his skin. The forest path opened before them, erasing itself behind them like a wound healing wrong. Dread pooled in his stomach as the cabin appeared.

The witch's anger crackled in the air as she muttered in that forbidden tongue. Her wand flicked, the door swung wide, and impossible space yawned inside. Cages stacked to a ceiling that shouldn't exist. So many children. His arms lowered the boy into another cage, gentle despite his inner screaming.

"They come to no harm." Leckermaul's voice carried false comfort. "I just need their Spark. It's the only way. You'll thank me when it's done. They'll get it back when they go home. We all will."

But he saw the empty eyes of the children in the cages. She had done that to them. Whatever she took, it couldn't possibly come back.

The witch circled the cages, trailing her fingers along the bars. Magic rippled in her wake, making the air thick and metallic. Inside him, Reuben's consciousness recoiled even as his body stood statue-still.

"The town remembers," she murmured, more to herself than him. "It's fighting back. That girl's charm—it calls to the old power." Her eyes gleamed fever bright. "Like your shifting does. Like these children's Spark."

He wanted to snarl, to shift, to tear her throat out with feline teeth. Instead, his body betrayed him with a calm nod.

"Soon." Her hand shot out, gripping his jaw. Foul magic burned where she touched him. "Soon I'll have enough Spark to break these walls. To remember what we really are."

The newest boy stirred in his cage. Reuben's heart thundered as Leckermaul approached, her wand weaving patterns that made his eyes water. Gold light seeped from the child's skin, gathering like mist around her hand.

"Beautiful," she breathed. The boy's color drained, vitality flowing into her waiting palm. "Each one brings me closer. Each Spark makes me stronger."

Reuben's inner scream matched the silence of the watching children. He knew he'd forget this horror until next time. But some part of him would remember—just like some part of Allison remembered whatever truth lay buried in this twisted town.

The witch's spell finished, leaving another empty-eyed child in its wake. She turned to him, smile sharp as broken glass. "Now, cat. Time to deliver our message. Let them find this one where the charm-bearer will see."

His body moved without permission, lifting the boy. Soon he'd wake up in some other part of town, with no memory of how he got there or what he'd done.

Just like the children.

Just like Allison.

Just like all of them, trapped in this town's deadly game of forget and remember.

Chapter Fourteen

THE CABIN IN THE WOODS

*I*f there was one thing Dee hoped to never see again, it was the inside of the Sueños Del Mar police station. Some of the people who worked inside might be lovely people, but she didn't care. She also never wanted to see any of them again. Especially the old man who never failed to show up everywhere.

Why was he everywhere?

Even though he did convince that obnoxious detective to give Allie the key they'd taken from the Thornes. Something about it not being what he was looking for? She couldn't quite remember what he said, though she did remember the extreme ire, borderline rage that rolled off the typically docile elderly man. It had set her heart racing, though she couldn't say why. The rage couldn't have been directed towards them, because they'd never done anything to him. They didn't even know his name.

Regardless, the key was returned to them, for all the good it did. If they knew what it was for, what lock it fit into, maybe it would have been worth returning to the Thornes. Otherwise, all it did was get them dragged into the police station again.

"Food?" Allie asked as they dragged themselves across the parking lot in the gray light of early dawn.

Honestly, it was a good thing they currently didn't have any active clients since they kept going without sleep due to time spent in the wretched Sueños Del Mar jail. Well, not *good*, but at least they would have time to catch up on sleep.

"Sure," Dee yawned. "Let's get food."

The Prius was impounded, but she'd think about that later. She'd have to get her aunt or uncle to go with her to pick it up. Which meant she'd have to explain to them why it was impounded. Which meant she'd have to talk to them, and considering she'd been dodging their calls for days, it wasn't something she looked forward to. Hence, the thinking about it later.

Suddenly, it occurred to her that she'd been away from home for hours. She hadn't put Kansas in his crate when they went to check out the Thornes, since she didn't know how long they would be gone. It wasn't always strictly necessary to crate him every time she left, but he had been out in the house overnight. There was no telling what type of mess she'd find. Her dog was almost perfect, but he was still a dog.

"You know what? You go. I need to get home and make sure Kansas is okay."

Allie linked an arm through Dee's. "Kansas is fine. He is a well-fed, well-behaved dog. You made sure he had plenty of water when we left yesterday. He will not starve if he has to wait another hour to eat his breakfast. We just spent another night in freaking jail. We deserve baked goods and fresh coffee."

"Can we make a pact to never spend another night in jail? Please?"

Allie laughed, the sound doing a lot to unwind the tension in Dee's shoulders. "I would like to say absolutely, but who knows? Maybe this is only the start of our life of crime."

"You were there, right? When you told me I wasn't cut out for a life of crime?"

"Yes, silly, but that was before you told me about the bathroom window."

"I'm pretty sure you were right with the original assessment. I don't have the constitution for this particular brand of excitement."

They stumbled along the sidewalk, turning on an empty Main Street, and managed the next couple blocks without running into another soul. One thing about Sueños Del Mar, the citizens were late risers. Or, at least, later than six in the morning. They'd never had a client call or appointment before nine thirty and even that was rare. Maybe the commuters were the early-rising types, she thought vaguely, having no idea where anyone would commute to. What was near Sueños Del Mar? Anything? Had she ever been outside her town?

She shook her head. How ridiculous. Why would she *need* to leave Sueños Del Mar? Everything was right here. The schools, the stores, the restaurants, and even a duck-pin bowling alley. She could walk along a beach and hike in a heavily wooded park all within a few miles. Unlike Allie, she had never considered leaving town.

The bakery came into view after another block. The day had lightened, but not enough to compete with the yellow warmth of the front windows. It drew them in, promising all the comforts the jail couldn't offer. Low bar, sure, but that didn't take away from the bakery's appeal.

"Is he always here?" Allie groaned, spotting Reuben behind the counter while also running her fingers first through her hair and then under her eyes.

"You're as beautiful as ever. Don't worry."

"I'm not," Allie replied flippantly. "Worried, I mean."

Dee swung the door open and then immediately wished she had also taken two seconds to set herself to rights. Leander sat, engulfing a small table in the corner with his hulking form. He was mid-sip of coffee when he spotted her, spilling his drink and nearly knocking the table over in his haste to stand.

"Dee! Shit. Uh." And quieter, "Shit."

"I always thought lions would be more graceful," Reuben pondered in a clearly amused voice.

"What's that mean?" Allie asked, ignoring the mess in the corner and instead focused on the goods behind the counter.

"Nothing," Lee growled, righting the table. "He's just," he waved a hand at himself, "being a jackass."

Dee swiped a handful of napkins and helped Leander mop up the coffee. "You're up early," she commented, dabbing at a spot of coffee on the tip of his worn boots. She liked that about him, that he was completely unpretentious. It was one of the things that initially drew her to him. At least, she paused, handful of soaked napkins held a couple inches above the floor, she thought it was one of the first things. She couldn't quite remember how they met, exactly. Was it—

"Are you okay?" Leander asked quietly, gathering the used napkins in his large hands. "I heard that cop picked you up again."

"Fine," she said brightly. "I'm fine." She stood, wiping her wet hands on her dirty jeans. "We just got out. Again. And we're hungry. And," she smiled, refusing to stop even though he was staring at her as if she had been body swapped. Like she couldn't be cheery. Like she should be in tears just because that was what she did the last time she got out of jail." And I need to wash my hands. So." She hurriedly stepped around him, but he caught her by the arm.

"Dee."

"I'm fine." She shook him off and continued towards the restroom, head held high for reasons she didn't understand. What was she doing and why was she doing it at that exact moment?

Ugh. Definitely should have taken a few moments to smooth her hair before stepping into the bakery. She hadn't bothered wearing makeup on the stakeout, but her hair was a fuzzy mess. She quickly smoothed and braided her hair, twisting the omni-present hairband from her wrist around the tail of the braid, splashed cold water on her face, and ran a wet finger over her teeth until they squeaked. Squaring her shoulders, she marched back into the dining area to find Allie and the two men—Leander sitting, Reuben standing next to Allie—at a table with two coffees and several baked goods, including strawberry strudel kuchen and puddingbrezel, a variety of rolls, and maybe even a pie or ... she dug in her memory for the name, loudly declaring, "Kreppel!"

Everyone turned in just enough time to see her cheeks blaze.

"Here. You sit." Leander leapt from the chair he occupied, holding it until she took his place, and then scooted her toward the table.

It was then she noticed the key sitting in the middle of the two steaming cups of coffee.

"I've seen this before," Reuben said, a strange, glassy look to his eyes. "I just," he shook his head. "I don't know where."

"Maybe if you held it?" Leander suggested, one hand still resting on the back of Dee's chair.

Reuben took a backward step. "No. Nope. I'm not touching it."

"Why not?" Allie picked it up. "It's just a key. There's literally nothing scary about it."

"I didn't say I was scared." But he retreated back behind the counter, where the dazed expression finally left his face and was replaced by the familiar insouciance. "But I don't like it. Don't want my fingerprints on it."

"I told them where we got it," Allie informed her. "He told us Thorne owns this building. She and Leckermaul do not get along. Surprise, surprise."

"What if you held it and then we wiped it down?" Lee suggested, pulling a chair over, positioning himself close enough to Dee that one of his knees touched hers, a small point of heat in an otherwise chilly morning. It was embarrassing to admit how much she liked having the contact, even if it was basically nothing, even if she was only admitting it to herself.

She took a scalding sip of black coffee, which also provided a point of heat as it burned its way down her throat.

"Why are you so bent on him holding the key?" Allie asked amused, pushing the puddingbrezel towards Dee, knowing it was her absolute favorite. She rarely got one, though, because they were always eating on the go, and it wouldn't look great to show up to a client's house with crumbs and vanilla custard all over her face.

"Because," Lee shrugged, eyeing the kreppel. "Is that good?"

Dee nudged his knee with hers. "It is. Would you like some of it?"

"Some?" Allie snorted, tearing apart a roll. "He's looking like he'd eat all of them."

"That's fine." Dee moved the plate in front of him. "You can have them."

He held her gaze, something passing through his eyes, something she wasn't sure she'd ever seen before. Something like yearning, only without the passion. He didn't look like a man who wanted *her* so much as he wanted *something* without knowing what that something was. Something more than kreppel.

Reuben groaned. "This is excruciating."

Allie giggled and then slapped a hand over her mouth.

For a few minutes, the only sounds were of the three of them eating while Reuben hovered behind the counter. Dee assumed the bakery would be busier at this time of the morning, but so far, they were still the only citizens out. Which was lucky, because she doubted Leander would have said, "Holding the key might jog your memory. Sometimes things are magical that way."

After a few more minutes of eating and some back-and-forth bickering, Reuben declared they should all go to the girls' house. He would close up since he hadn't seen Leckermaul in days to his memory and he was tired of doing all the work for the old witch. He'd feel better studying the key in private and maybe Leander would be right. Holding the key might jog his memory, and, if so, they could brainstorm on... Well, he didn't know what they could brainstorm until he figured out where he'd seen the key before and what it unlocked.

～

*K*ansas nearly bowled her over as soon as they walked through the door, Rabbit yowling from the top of the stairs, but both animals were alive, and Dee swore she would never leave them alone that long again.

"You should have called me." Leander followed close at her heels as she fed the dog and refreshed the water. "I would have taken care of them."

"You were busy, weren't you? Fixing the Thornes' car or whatever. How'd that go?" Under no circumstances would she be calling him from jail. Ever.

"Fine. It was a ... dent. No big deal." He stopped her at the sink after she washed her hands, turning her to face him. "Did you want to shower or anything?"

"Are you saying I need to?"

His smile was standard issue, laid back Leander. She felt like it had been missing ever since he'd picked them up after the first night in jail. She'd missed it, to be honest, and seeing it now went a long way toward convincing her life would be okay. Leander was still chill, the culprit would be found, and...

"Oh, no," she shouted at the same time Reuben let himself in through the back door. "Another kid was taken last night."

"That's right," Allie confirmed, coming back downstairs after performing the world's fastest wardrobe change out of the black of the stakeout and into a pair of pale blue knit pants and a white tee, hair brushed out, and skin glowing. "Susan Glenda said something about that last night."

"They didn't even question us about it. That's got to be a good sign, right?"

Everyone agreed it was, and with that happy thought, Dee escaped upstairs to do her own wardrobe change, complete with brushing her teeth and another rebraiding. So, after Reuben held the key in a loose grip, his eyes going fuzzy and far away, his body swaying from side to side until Dee was certain he'd fall off his chair, and he declared, "I know where to go," she was ready to walk out the door. Allie, around the world's largest yawn, muttered something about putting on something less comfortable to go on a magic adventure, and then they were off in Leander's truck, Dee stretching out across the small bench in the crew cab with Rueben in the passenger seat, and Allie between the two men, toward the woods that surrounded Sueños Del Mar.

Stepping out into a gravel lot, plants on the verge of taking over in all the places between tire treads, and surrounded by ancient firs and spruce towering several yards above their heads, she could imagine there was magic in the world. The forest whispered to her about other, older worlds, pulling her with some unnamed lure.

Magic. Her brain supplied the word in a hushed, reverent tone, if brains could do that inside one's own head.

Like the old man who was everywhere or Allie's charm bracelet that turned everyone who saw it slightly feral or how an old iron key could jog the memory of an exceptionally attractive bakery assistant enough for him to lead them into an ancient forest looking for who knew what. Their world held magic, and she had somehow never noticed it before.

Before talking herself out of it, she reached for Leander's hand, comforted when he didn't hesitate to thread his fingers through hers.

"It'll be all right, Dorseigh," he murmured. "I think we can trust him."

That "think" was doing an awful lot of heavy lifting in Dee's opinion.

Reuben stood alone, a few feet away, turning in a slow circle, like a water witch with a dowsing rod, until he found what he was looking for. A signal? A familiar landmark? A lure?

It was a trap, she thought, her hand squeezing Lee's, but she followed the strange man into the woods. They all did without a hint of hesitation.

The cabin was in the woods. Deep, yes, but not as deep as a secret cabin in the woods should be. In Dee's mind, if something was going to be hidden, it should take at least a couple of hours to find. They had only followed Reuben for maybe twenty minutes. Maybe it helped that he seemed to know exactly where to go? Still, him leading them directly there did nothing to quell her suspicions of a trap.

The trees stopped only a few steps before the plain wooden door and would give them cover as they tried to sneak up. Reuben slunk from tree to tree, having chosen a route that kept him in the shadows and out of sight of the two windows set in the front of the cabin. His fluid movement reminded her of Rabbit, which was silly. A grown man was nothing like a cat.

Because he navigated the distance so much easier than the rest of them, he was the one who hit a barrier, jolting backwards, yelping out a curse.

"What was that?" Leander hissed.

"How should I know?" He shook at his arm, grimacing. "Something zapped me."

Allie crept up behind him, daring to reach around, searching for whatever he'd walked into, but didn't manage to touch anything. Reuben gently pushed her backward.

"There's no reason for you to hurt yourself, lovely." His grin was tight lipped and just a little bit strained.

"But—"

"I'll do it." Leander released Dee's hand and strode forward four steps before he smacked into the same barrier, falling on his ass, his long hair practically standing on end. "Ow."

"What is it? I don't see anything." Dee squatted, picking up a rock, and tossing it towards the cabin. One second later, it plunked against the door.

Lee flopped onto his back with a grunt. "I'll just be here if you need anything."

"Maybe it's like an invisible fence?" Allie suggested, retreating a few steps from Reuben, distancing herself from the probability of getting zapped.

"I don't think that's how it works." Dee lay on her belly, stretching forward only as far as Leander's feet, looking for any sign of fencing or wires, anything that would explain what prevented them from getting closer to the cabin. "Maybe it's only here in front. We can circle around to the back and check?"

"If you are suggesting we try walking into that again, I vote nay." Reuben rubbed at his arm. "I think ... but ... I *know* I've been here before. I just can't—"

"Maybe we should call the police," Allie said, cutting him off. "Then they can deal with it."

"And tell them what?" Dee asked, nose nearly pressed to the ground. "That there is a cabin in the woods and the key we stole from the Thornes might open it?"

"Well, maybe not that exactly, but something close. We don't have to tell them who we are."

Strong hands gripped Dee's hips, hauling her backward, Leander setting her on her butt beside him. He was a little pale under the tawny scruff, a long red blister beginning to bubble up on his forehead. "Sorry," he mumbled. "No reason for you to injure yourself, either."

When they'd entered the forest, it was still a damp, chilly morning, but now the sun was up, the fog had dissipated, and heat began seeping in through the canopy of trees. Nothing too overwhelming, but enough to cause a layer of sweat to break out on Dee's forehead and lip. Frustration built along with the heat. The cabin was *right there* but they couldn't touch it. Something about it, about an invisible barrier, about Allie's charm, the old man, the missing kids, all of it, sat uneasy in Dee's stomach. Things were happening that she didn't understand, and the more she looked at the situation, the more she thought she should *stop*. Whatever they found would change them, and she wasn't sure if it would be for the better.

"Let's go back home. We can eat lunch and regroup."

"And call the police?" Allie asked, hopefully.

Dee sighed. "Sure. Let's go call the police."

Chapter Fifteen

PUT A SPELL ON YOU

he cabin's lingering magic made Allie's skin crawl. She'd
perfected the vapid rich-girl act, a mask that had saved her
more than once. After all, who'd believe some ditzy socialite could
steal a watch, fight off an attacker, or... No. She wouldn't think about
that day on the overpass.

She'd almost slipped up then like she had that night, leaving a
digital trail. Her phone had tracked every movement, every awful
moment. At least now her brain was working ahead of her fear.

Reuben squeezed into the truck with them, his presence both
comforting and unsettling. "So what's the plan?"

Their eyes met in the rearview mirror. She recognized that look—
someone else carrying secrets that burned to be told. What darkness
lurked behind his easy smile? For a moment she wondered if he was
behind it all, but her gut said no. She knew performative cheerfulness;
she'd mastered it. But the guilt in his eyes when he looked at the
cabin? That was real.

"Can't use our phones," she said. "They'll track us."

The truck's atmosphere turned heavy until Dee spoke up. "We
need burner phones."

Allie turned to stare at her friend. "Since when do you know about burner phones?"

"Some of us watch crime shows instead of dating." Dee's pointed comment made Leander choke on air.

His face flamed as he started the engine. "I know where to go."

"Perfect." Reuben's grin carried an edge of mania. "It's like a heist movie with rom-com elements."

"Who's the couple?" Dee asked, deadpan despite her matching blush.

"Me and Allie, obviously."

Allison's traitorous heart stuttered. He was joking, had to be.

Leander guided them into the town's seedier side—liquor stores, vape shops, men loitering with electronic cigarettes glowing in the growing dark. For Sueños Del Mar, this was as dangerous as it got. Before the disappearances, even this neighborhood had been postcard perfect. Something was changing about this already stifling town. Something sinister.

"Lovely ambiance," Allie muttered, sarcasm hiding her fear as always.

Dee threw up her hands. "Exactly where my life's headed. Hanging with miscreants and criminals."

"Real criminals don't say 'miscreants,'" Reuben pointed out.

"I've seen them here." Leander nodded toward the gas station. Leave it to the big softie to know the only legitimate business on the block. "Who's going in?"

"Not all of us." Dee's voice carried new steel. "We don't need witnesses."

Allie grabbed Leander's hat from the back, grimacing at the motor oil smell. She tied her hair up and slid on sunglasses despite the darkness. "I'll go. Drive around, keep my phone away from here. Fifteen minutes, four blocks north." She held out her hand. "Cash?"

The boys complied, but Reuben's eyes held a warning she couldn't quite read. Something about this place made her charm bracelet feel heavy, like it knew things she didn't.

Inside, cheap fluorescent lights hummed overhead as she

approached the burner phone display. One more tool for survival, one more step toward answers.

Inside, the young man behind the counter smiled broadly as she approached. His eyes roamed over her salaciously and then he asked in a half-joking tone. "You're too pretty to be from around here. Are you a movie star or something?"

Although she'd normally hand him a card for her streaming page or tell him to fuck off, this was the first time in a while that someone didn't act like she was a child-abducting pariah, and it made her a little happy and a lot reckless. Allie flashed her webcam smile at him, pulling down the sunglasses to wink. "Something like that."

"Oh, whoa. You're-you're—" He pointed at her with one hand and knocked off his baseball cap with the other as he wiped his hand over his head. The young man was in such a state of shock he didn't even notice he'd done it. He only gaped and stammered.

Her stomach knotted. *Damn it. Should have kept the glasses on!* After shoving the burner phone onto the counter, she crossed her arms over her chest. "Yeah. It's me. Can you just ring me up? I'm kinda in a hurry."

He shook his head. "No. I can't do that."

Incredulous, she reared her head. "No? Are you refusing me service?"

His cheeks flushed crimson, and he held up his hands as if surrendering. "No! The opposite. I'm a subscriber ... well, I was before... You know ... the news."

She screamed internally. Outwardly, she crossed her arms across her chest.

Noticing her defensiveness, he blew out his breath. "I'm messing this up. I'm a big fan and believe that you're innocent. You were home. It was all on camera. I don't believe the rumors that you ran pre-recorded footage. The clothes were different every night. Some of us even noted the way the light changed, and your cat's patterns of movement didn't loop."

She stared. The streaming channel that was taken down was proof she was innocent. But where did that leave Dee? Could she be Dee's alibi if she were sleeping? It would be worth asking the lawyer. She'd have to sticky note that thought. First, she needed to report Lecker-maul. Catching the possible culprit was her best defense.

The cashier cleared his throat. "S-sorry I'm rambling. I've missed you—your channel. Let me at least pay for this." He rang up the burner and paid with cash. Then he fished a cell phone out of his jeans with shaky hands. "Can I get a selfie with you?"

Eyes on the burner he still held in his other hand, she gnawed her bottom lip. "Yeah. Only if you promise to only show it to your friends. No socials. I'm trying to be low key until the real kidnapper is found."

"I swear. It's just for me anyway." He grinned furiously at her. "My situationship is kinda jealous of you, but I've told her that we're not official. I'm free to date whoever I want."

Allie ignored the icky feeling the creepy flirtation left her with. She just wanted the dang burner phone and to leave, but she also wanted her fans on her side. That income meant getting out of this town after this was all over. "Cool. Um, I'm kinda in a hurry."

He straightened. "Right. Sorry."

The cashier made his way around and snapped a selfie of the two of them with his arm around Allie. Even with sunglasses and a hat, she appeared annoyed to be in the photograph, and not really like herself. Still, the dude thanked her profusely for letting him have a pic. His gratitude trailed after her as she bolted with the burner cell phone out the door.

Allie called the police station. A desk cop answered in a bored tone, "Sueños Del Mar police department."

"I'd like to report suspicious activity that might be tied to the kidnappings."

"What's your name?"

"I'd like to keep this anonymous."

"Look, I'll take down your information, but it won't be taken seriously without a name. We've got all kinds of weirdos claiming they've seen a witch climbing the sides of houses like Santa and flying off in the night. If you want to report anything like that, I'll write it down because it's my job, but you need some help, and it's not the kind the police can provide."

She swallowed hard. "No. Nothing like that. I think I heard kids shouting for help when I was on a run."

There was some scrambling on the other end. "Where and when?"

"Just now."

After giving the police officer details, he asked her to hold. Allie wasn't an idiot. She knew he'd put the detective in charge on, and that cop knew her voice by now. She agreed but hung up and then smashed the phone with the heel of her shoe and dumped the bits in different trash cans and bins along the way.

About ten minutes later she found Leander's truck idling in a parking lot. Allie hopped in. "It's done." Noticing only Dee was there sporting a worried look, she turned around fully scanning the lot for the two men, then returned her gaze to her roommate. "Where did Reuben and Lee go?"

Dee frowned. "Reuben did the sleepwalking thing again. Lee followed. I stayed behind so you'd know what happened." Her voice trembled as she continued, "Something is really wrong. He couldn't even answer us. It was like–" she paused as if weighing her words. "Have you ever seen those old movies where someone is under hypnosis or..."

"Or under a spell?" Allie asked what Dee seemed to be having trouble saying out loud.

She nodded furiously, her blue eyes widening as large as Elijah Woods's peepers in those *Lord of the Rings* movies. "He looked like a marionette, and someone was pulling his strings."

Allie climbed into Lee's seat and buckled up. "Well, let's save Pinocchio."

After driving for ten minutes down the street where Dee last saw them, Leander and Reuben were nowhere to be found. "Where do you think they went?" Part of her knew where they'd gone but didn't want to think this was an actual case of an old lady with magical powers over Reuben.

Dee's phone dinged. She looked at the screen. "Lee sent me his location. The map is tracking their movement. Holy crap. They're moving fast."

With Dee's directions and some quick maneuvering on Allie's part, they finally caught up with the two guys. She spotted Lee's big form first. Leander usually moved slowly and didn't seem to be the type with a great amount of agility. The large man moved with the grace of an Olympian as he chased Reuben to an apartment complex.

Allie and Dee got out and joined Leander watching Reuben clamber up a wall.

"He looks like one of those parkour guys," Lee remarked.

Allie gasped as the dark figure of Reuben swung from one precarious perch to another. Dee squeezed her hand. "Should we stop Spiderman?"

Leander stretched and then stroked his chin. "Nah. I tackled him, and he threw me off like I was a rag doll. The lights are on, but nobody's home."

Allie squeezed Dee's hand back and then withdrew to fold her arms across her chest. "Things are getting weirder and weirder."

Leander gave her a nod. He spoke in a low, conspiratorial tone. "Nothing about this town is right—especially the people. I think—I think it's time that we all talk about a few things."

A frisson slithered up her spine like a cold, wet snake. Sometimes online, the conspiracy theorists would say they were living in a simulation. That their world wasn't real. They weren't real. Some said that they lived in a mirror world and that another world was out there with copies of themselves. Every time she'd read the theories, her stomach would flip flop.

If it were true. There would be no escape for her. Still, part of her wanted to know why she'd wanted to leave, even before the Bad Day.

"Um, guys?" Dee spoke in a voice a few octaves higher than usual, breaking Allison out of her spiral. "He's trying to break into that window." She turned to Lee gesturing at the building. "*Do* something."

Lee cursed and sprinted with preternatural speed at the apartment complex. He leapt, clearing at least ten feet, and landed on the rail of a balcony. There, he perched as if he were a Cirque du Soleil performer. No. No performer could clear the first floor without a trampoline or springboard.

"How the hell did he do that?"

Dee slapped a hand over her gaping mouth, and her eyes grew round as planets. She shook her head, unable to speak.

Lee squatted and then did it again and again until he was on the fourth-floor balcony. Dee yipped. Every. Single. Time. Which, Allie would have thought was cute if they weren't in a seriously fucked scenario.

Reuben had spider-monkeyed over to a window and was clawing at the frame, trying to open it. He looked more like an apparition from a horror movie than the cute bakery assistant who gave her extra pastries and smiled too much.

Allie scowled. She had dated a guy that turned out to be all flash and no cash that lived in one of the buildings. The windows locked from the inside. He wasn't going to get it open. Why was he even trying?

At that moment, Leander sprang, reminding her of a jungle cat taking down a gazelle in a nature show.

Her heart shot into her throat as the two men tumbled to the ground. Before she realized what she was doing, she was running toward them. So was Dee.

Leander looked up, dazed. Reuben wasn't moving at all.

"Is he dead?" Allie asked in a harsh whisper, fear making her voice shake.

"Nah. It'd take much more than that to kill him." Lee pushed to his feet and slung Reuben's limp body over his shoulder. "He's out cold though. Given he was clawing at some poor half-awake kid's window might be the best thing for him. Let's get out of here before someone calls the cops."

Chapter Sixteen

TRUST

"*Do something.*"

His heart pounded hard enough to vibrate his teeth. He couldn't do anything, not without giving himself away.

It had been years since he first shifted, years since he'd learned he was different and had successfully kept it to himself. All the way up until he turned into a lion in the middle of the day and ran over a car. The girls didn't know about that. The girls *could not* know about that. They'd know he was different and not in a fun way. Not in a "Oh, he has a weird quirk but is still a nice fully human man" way. They would know he was a freak. That he was bad different. Weird different. Inhuman different. How could it be any other way? He *was* different. He grew fur and teeth and claws. He was about as different as it could get.

But, Dee had asked him. Demanded, more like. And even if she didn't know it, he would do just about anything for her. With a curse, he sprinted toward the lowest balcony, squatted enough to gather his strength, and launched himself upward. He easily caught the railing, sending a quick prayer into the universe that it would hold his weight before swinging himself over. He wouldn't allow himself to look down.

Dee was down there, for one thing, and he didn't want to know what she thought of this display. He probably looked like a lumbering oaf next to Reuben, who had jumped from balcony to balcony like it was no big deal.

For him, it was a very big deal. He had at least fifty pounds on the other man. He grimaced and leapt up to the next balcony. Or more like seventy. The stupid cat was lithe and lean, and Leander was not either of those things.

The railing of the balcony below Reuben groaned, pulling away from the brick wall just a little when Leander landed on it. He wobbled, ignoring a quick jab of fear, and then he was finally on the balcony next to Reuben. The other man was several feet away, perched on a six-inch ledge, pounding on a window in a blind rage.

Leander could just make out the inside of the room where a boy sat in his bed, blinking at them through the growing darkness. He just knew the kid was going to start screaming for his mom at any second.

"Shit. Let's go, asshole." There was no way to get down but to jump, and he knew Reuben would not go willingly. Whoever had him in their grasp wasn't going to release him without a fight. That was fine, Leander guessed, squaring his shoulders. He was used to doing things the hard way.

He leapt one final time, catching Reuben by the shoulders, both of them falling to the ground below. Leander clutched Reuben, twisting himself around so that he'd land on his back with the other man on top of him. He didn't know if the cat healed easily, but he sure didn't want to be responsible for crushing him either way.

The ground came up fast, and he landed poorly on his left shoulder, the wind temporarily knocked from his lungs. He rolled Reuben off just in time for the girls to run up.

Allie asked if the other man was dead. No one asked about him at all. Which figured. Big lumbering oafs like him were probably always fine. He pushed himself up, teeth gritted against the protestation of all his bones. Somehow, miraculously, nothing seemed to be broken, and other than his throbbing, possibly dislocated shoulder, his body was in working order. Sirens screamed to life in the distance, not close enough for the girls to hear, but he could. Recovery would have to wait. Instead, he slung the unconscious Reuben over his good shoulder and headed to his truck.

~

*T*hey made it halfway to the truck when the sirens started. Sueños Del Mar wasn't a large city by any stretch of the imagination, but hearing the sirens meant the police were closer than Dee was comfortable with. The police station was far enough away that they wouldn't be able to hear it from where they ran through a maze of apartment buildings. Which meant, of course, they needed to get out of there. She urged her companions to hurry, to move faster. They had to disappear before they crossed any of the apartment residents or were seen fleeing by anyone looking out the multitude of surrounding windows. Leander's truck wasn't some new, blend-in-with-the-crowd style. It wasn't as old as Bertha, but it sure wasn't a flashy new model that looked like all the other flashy new models. She wouldn't feel safe until the apartment buildings were far away in the rearview mirror and no one could place them at the scene of an attempted break-in.

"Put him in the back," Allie whisper-shouted once they were finally at Leander's truck, flinging open the door for Lee to toss the unconscious man inside.

If they weren't literally running for their lives, Dee might have said something about the way Allie slid into the cramped space beside Reuben, gently taking his head into her lap. She'd never known Allie to care about the looks of any man more than she cared about the size of his bank account. Maybe she was ready to start? Now wasn't the time to ask, that was for sure.

Leander, once unloaded of his burden, seemed to have decided the danger had passed. He pushed back the seat, buckled up, arranged the mirrors, even used the turn-signal when easing out of the apartment's lot. Dee bit her tongue for one entire block as the truck moseyed along at five miles under the speed limit, but then, finally, she couldn't take it anymore.

"What the fuck is going on?" She breathed, staring straight at the side of Leander's head, impossible to miss his shoulders jumping up to his ears at the harshness of her question.

Allie whistled. "Someone's pissed. Actually," she kicked the back of Leander's seat, "make that two someones."

"Uh, what do you mean?"

Dorseigh Gale, certified good girl, the solver of problems, the bearer of guilt, snarled, a sound no one on the green earth had ever heard come out of her. "What I mean is, what the *fuck* is going on?" She pushed at his shoulder, his flinch raising her ire. She hated when he did this, when he would suddenly flip from the easy-going, laid-back man she knew into someone who feared her. *Her*! No one was afraid of her and with good reason. She wasn't scary. She was the least scary person she knew!

The first time it'd happened, the first time he showed irrational fear, was shortly after they'd first met. She was wearing a new blue dress. Her waves lay perfectly against her head. She'd had on make-up. She'd felt as cute as she ever had, confidence high, spirits higher. She'd seen him walking toward her, probably headed to his newly opened shop. They weren't friends yet, but they were something one step above acquaintances. Honestly, she still didn't know what gave her the courage, but she'd asked him out. Just lunch, something casual. And he'd frozen like prey, like she was the predator. Which was ridiculous, because, again, no one was afraid of her. She was too nice, too friendly, too accommodating. So, of course, as she listened to him mumble and stumble over plausible excuses, she'd saved him, waving it away, saying it was no big deal, it was a silly suggestion.

She'd never asked again. Obviously. She wasn't stupid. Clearly the thought of going on a date with her was the most terrifying thing he could think of. It made her question everything about herself then, but not now. Now it burrowed under her skin.

"Why are you flinching? Just answer the question."

He licked his lips, both hands flexing around the steering wheel. For a second, Dee imagined there were claws on the tips of his fingers. Then she blinked and the illusion was gone.

"I told Allison. Did you tell her what happened?" He asked, his eyes darting up to the rearview mirror and away.

"I sure did," Allie replied in a sing-song voice that Dee knew she used only when she was deeply and violently irritated. She used to talk to Thorne using the sing-song voice. The sing-song voice was a harbinger of worse tempers to come.

"I'm not talking about the possessed puppet man. We'll ask him once he wakes up. I'm talking about you, Leander. You bounced up the side of that building like it was nothing! Like, you often go around scaling buildings. And then, you both fell without any injuries. You, like, jumped right up after falling off a building and carried a fully-grown man over one shoulder like it was *nothing*. That's not normal, Leander! None of this makes any sense. Not the police. Not the kids. Not Mrs. Leckermaul looking actual decades younger than she did two weeks ago! None of it. There's a cabin in the woods that has some sort of force-field around it, the Thorne's have a dragon—"

"Jabberwocky."

"A jabberwocky-themed sex room and no food in their house! There's a weird key. There's a lawyer who won't officially represent us but apparently wants to still be involved because she seems to hate the police. And then there's you! You have been all over this mess with us and why? Why, Leander? We aren't that good of friends. In fact, I don't even know if you like me. Us. Do you even like us? And you climb buildings fearlessly, but now you're acting all timid and cowardly, like I'm going to hurt you! When have I ever hurt you?"

"And jump from buildings," Allie added, off-handedly. "Let's not forget that jump. So effortless! So agile. Anyone ever tell you you're pretty agile for a large man?"

"So, what's going on? You seem to know something. You said we should talk. Let's talk."

"Here?" He squeaked before clearing his throat and saying in a normal voice, "I don't think right now is the best time." He shot her an injured look, so at least there was that.

"Oh, I do. I think we have got *nothing* but time right now."

"Where are we, anyway?" Allie leaned over the bench seat. "And what are we going to do about Reuben? This shit is messed up, but I don't want him to die on us. Can we at least take him to the hospital?"

Dee stared expectantly at Leander.

"I don't—" He scrubbed a hand down his face. "I'm just driving. I don't have any destination in mind. Do you?" He dared a glance at Dee. And then to Allie he said, "He'll be fine. I'm the one he landed on."

"What is going on?" Dee asked as gently as her raised blood pressure allowed. She couldn't hang on to her anger. She knew from experience she couldn't. Raising her voice and cursing at him was more than she generally allowed. No one would want to trust a person who raised their voice. Or, at least, they don't feel *safe* about it. She wanted to be a safe person, even when she was angry.

"I..." He sighed, turning toward the forest that ringed the town. "I can't do that, not completely. It's not my story, and I don't know all of it, anyway. Not ... not completely. But," he held up a hand when Dee started to protest. "I'll tell you that there's a lot more to this place than you know. There's more to, to me, and to Reuben, and to a lot of the residents."

"What does that mean?" Dee asked, exasperated. He was saying words, none of which had any firm meaning. She needed firm! Almost more than anything else.

"It means that there's stuff happening that is above my pay grade," he said, equally exasperated. "I don't know everything, Dee. I just know people don't act like Reuben did earlier and that there are things about me that I don't understand either. I'll tell you, okay? I will." He audibly swallowed. "But not right now. I need more time."

"I think that's a whole lot of bullshit, Lee, just so you're all clear where I stand." Allie patted him on the back. "I don't hear the sirens anymore."

"Great," Dee said, not feeling as angry, but not quite ready to let the oddness of the evening go. "So, you're probably fine to tell us something. You haven't explained anything. You just said stuff we already know. The town is weird? If we didn't know that before, we definitely do now. So, don't tell me everything, but at least tell us one thing. Just one. Explain how you climbed up the balconies. How it is that you can jump ten feet straight up and land on a railing. Just explain that one thing."

After a few long seconds, he mumbled, "I have, um, some abilities."

"Abilities?" Dee drawled the word out to several syllables. "You are unbelievable. Can you just take us home?"

"What about Reuben? What are we going to do with him? What if he wakes up and takes off again?" Allie's fingers dug into Dee's shoulder. "We can't just leave him."

"I don't know." Dee rubbed her temples. Full night had finally fallen. She was exhausted. How many nights had it been since she'd had a good sleep? Since the first night in custody, she assumed, but it might be longer than that. The nightmares about her past had been more frequent lately, ramping up like never before. Most nights had at least one moment where she was drenched in sweat and waking herself up with a scream. Her entire world was spinning out of control. She wanted just one thing to make sense. Just one, but Leander wasn't going to give that to her, no matter how many nightmares she had, no matter how guilty she felt about everything; about not calling her aunt and uncle more, about avoiding them, about the Prius being stuck in the police impound.

Ugh. How was she going to explain why the Prius was impounded?

"I might have a plan," Leander said quietly. "If you trust me, I think I have a plan."

If they trusted him? Before the last hour, she would have said of course she trusted him. He was one of the only people she trusted. But, now? With him being cagey, with the dodged questions, and not giving a single straight answer? She found trust to be a little hard to come by.

"Dorseigh," he said, a big hand landing on her knee shooting a jolt of electricity up her leg, like when she kissed that one guy in high school, she'd had a crush on for months. That kiss had dazzled her for days. She swore her lips tingled with the sensation of his mouth on hers. Never mind that it wasn't a real kiss. A few of them were playing games and they matched. He *had* to kiss her. Still, it'd been a good kiss. "I promise you can trust me. I would never do anything to ruin our friendship."

Oh, hooray! Their friendship was intact.

She sighed. Her unrequited infatuation was not his concern. She wanted his friendship. Of course she did, even if sometimes she really needed more than his friendship, too.

"Fine. I trust you. What's your plan?"

"Everyone buckled up?" he asked, the truck shuddering as they accelerated.

"What?" Allie shrieked? "No! And Reuben isn't either."

Reuben groaned, as if in agreement.

"Keep hold of him, but strap yourself in," Leander said grimly.

"There are no seatbelts back here, you overgrown neanderthal," Allie shouted.

"Then hold on to something," Leander growled in a deep, un-Leander-like voice.

Dee searched the road as far as the old truck's headlights would show. She didn't see anything out of place. She didn't come to this park often but knew the road they were on led out of town. Maybe a night somewhere else would be a great way for them to regroup. They could sleep and lock Reuben in the bathtub, so he couldn't escape and go out looking for another apartment to break into.

"Where will we go?"

"Nowhere. You'll," he shook his head. "No, you won't see, but that doesn't matter. I think I can reset the last few hours. It's worked before, and I think it'll work with all of us in the truck."

"What are you talking about? Resetting the last few hours?"

"Are you ready?" he asked, eyes locked on the empty road ahead, pushing the truck harder until the shuddering shook her teeth.

The sign thanking people for visiting Sueños Del Mar sped towards them, Leander's hands tightened on the wheel, and Dee stared at him in bafflement. He acted like they were speeding towards their death. He acted like—

From the corner of her eye, Dee caught Reuben flinging himself upright, slamming against the back door. He screamed, "Stop!" punching the window hard enough to shatter the glass and then the entire world flashed bright white, blinding her, the seatbelt across her chest tightened painfully, her head flying forward even as the rest of her body mostly stayed in place. Someone screamed again. She thought she heard Leander apologize. She thought Reuben shouted something nonsensical, with a heavy British accent. And then the white light turned black, and she didn't know anything else.

Chapter Seventeen

CONTROL ALT DELETE

*R*euben pounded his fist on the door to the shop. The wood and metal shook with the ferocity of his knock.

"All right. All right! I'm coming. Gimme a sec!" Lee uncharacteristically grumbled from the other side. A series of deadbolts slid, and locks clicked before the door swung open.

"Why does a lion need so many freaking locks?" Reuben demanded.

The big man's eyes widened. Lee shook his head, hair tossing about like a mane, and then he said, "You're awake."

"Observant." He threw up his hands in frustration. "We were at the girls' house, and then I woke up in my bed. Care to fill me in on what happened in the meantime?"

The lion frowned. Then he looked like he was working on advanced Calculus. Reuben doubted the dude ever had to think very hard in his life. "I'm not asking for a Pulitzer-winning essay, King of the Jungle. Just the facts."

A ball of dread weighed heavy in his gut. He'd lost more time, and Lee obviously didn't want to share what he'd done while sleepwalking. Reuben hung his head but then forced himself to meet the other man's gaze—if they were men, that was. He didn't really know what he'd call the two of them. Were-animals seemed too cheesy ... yet werewolves in movies lost time. That didn't explain why he was most of the time conscious of when he walked around furry and with four legs. He perceived things differently, but he was still himself.

After wiping a massive hand over his face, Lee moved out of the door frame, giving just enough space for Reuben to pass. He swept a long arm to the front of his shop. "Best we discuss it inside."

~

*A*llison's temples throbbed to the beat of her slow and steady pulse. Her mouth felt like an arid wasteland and grit coated her teeth as she ran her tongue over them. Rarely, she fell asleep without brushing her teeth—as in since middle school, rarely. Her lashes seemed glued together when she dared to open her eyes. Unless a date plied her with drinks, she avoided alcohol but this sure felt like a hangover from her party girl days.

That was a lifetime ago.

Eons, really.

Before rent and responsibility made partying too difficult, before she had seen a comatose kid in her driveway and the inside of a jail cell. Part of her hoped she'd wake up in her private school dorm room. All of the past nine years would be a terrible nightmare, where she hadn't yet dated the bastard that ruined her life the first time, and her future was ... well, not whatever the hell was going on now.

Rubbing the gunk from her eyes, Allie managed to sit up and wake fully. Her stomach cramping, she prayed that the charm she'd swallowed showed up this morning. Also, dread of what she'd needed to do to retrieve it lingered with that feeling.

Rabbit jumped off the bed and waited by her door. He mewed and then began pawing the frame.

"Yes, sweet sweet. I know you're hungry."

Allie had a hard time recollecting what day it was and had a vague thought she should check her phone. At the prospect of a hundred notifications from people on social media in support of or against her case regarding the abductions, the thought got tossed. She opened the door, letting the cat out.

Dee's voice carried up the stairs. She was singing a country song. Midwest pop? Allie had no idea other than she didn't know the tune. The smell of frying pork products, also wafting up, caused her stomach to growl despite her growing urgency to use the toilet. Bodies were weird, she thought, as she stumbled her way down the hall to the bathroom.

Rabbit expected this as routine and followed. Standing with her hand on the doorknob, she looked down at the cat making infinity loops around and between her legs, and she sighed. "Are you sure you want to follow? This isn't going to be pretty."

The cat ignored her, scurrying into the bathroom as if treats awaited him there. No treats. No treats at all. Sometime later, she and Rabbit both regretted their previous choices, but Allie had a thoroughly cleaned and sanitized_charm to latch onto her charm bracelet.

"There you go." She glanced at Rabbit, who was stretched across the windowsill, grooming himself in the early morning sunshine. "Let's never speak of this again."

Looking in the mirror, she expected to see dark circles and for her skin to appear wan, but her cheeks were rosy, and her skin retained a healthy glow. Not a single blemish had ever marred her skin. Come to think of it, she never got scars from cuts either. She couldn't remember her hair ever looking bad. Didn't people have bad hair days? Hers always appeared artfully tousled when it wasn't brushed. Even her teeth sparkled white when she examined them in the mirror despite *feeling* gritty.

"Strange," she whispered, watching her reflection mime the word. Nothing here was right. The water felt real enough on her toothbrush, the bristles sharp against her gums, but reality seemed tissue thin. Like a game she couldn't quit.

Memories flooded back: Reuben's vacant eyes, Leckermaul's impossible cabin, men scaling buildings like spiders. The gaps in her memory felt deliberate now, carved out with surgical precision. How had she gotten from Lee's truck to her bed?

"Holy shit!" Dee's voice carried up the stairs, sharp with fear. "Allie?"

Kansas's bark held a warning she'd never heard before.

She bolted downstairs, nearly trampling Rabbit in her rush. In the kitchen, she found Dee trying to calm Kansas with treats, but the dog's whine carried an almost human desperation.

Even now, Dee looked perfect - not a hair out of place, her girl-next-door beauty unmarred by fear. Like a doll. Like they all were.

"I remember," Dee whispered into Kansas's fur. "We should be in Lee's truck. Running. What happened to us, Allie?"

The raw hurt in her voice made Allie's chest ache. Dee, solid as bedrock, was crumbling. Her small-town dreams of a life with Lee, of building something real in this unreal place, lay shattered at their feet. If Lee and Reuben had betrayed them—if any of this was their doing— Allie would burn it all down. Leckermaul, Thorne, that creeping detective, the old man with his pocket watch. Nobody used her friend like they'd used her. Dee asked for so little—just honesty, just half the bills. In Allie's world of users and takers, that simple trust meant everything.

"Everyone has secrets," Allie said, smoothing Dee's too-perfect waves. "But if Lee's behind this—"

"How far down this rabbit hole are you willing to go?" Her friend's eyes held a new steel.

Allie's grin felt feral. "With you? All the way to wonderland and back." Kansas's ears pricked. A knock came—three precise taps, just like the night they'd found the boy. They exchanged looks.

Whatever game this was, the next round had begun.

"Where do we say we were yesterday?" Allie whispered.

The dog growled low and then ran to the front of the house, barking. Dee gave the tail end of her dog a worried glance. Then she straightened. "Berry picking. We didn't find much and decided to read by the lake," she decided in hushed tones, not that anyone could hear anything over Kansas's ruckus.

"Specific. I like it." Allie pushed to her feet, offering a hand. Dee took it, and they headed down the hall, still holding hands. Unified in purpose.

At the door, her roommate let go to get a hand on Kansas's collar, quieting the pooch. That left it up to Allison to unlock and open the door. With her heart hammering in her chest, she did so.

Outside, a few feet back from the entrance at the precipice of where the front porch ended, Detective Doyle waited. The plants in pots from various thrifting and yard sale finds flanked him on either side. They caught him in the middle of examining one of the plants. The foliage paired with the detective's handlebar mustache, hair slicked back with pomade, and outfit consisting of a white button down, vest, blazer, and trousers gave Doyle the appearance of a botanist ... or perhaps an archaeologist from a movie set in the past. Not Indiana Jones, but further back.

To her surprise, Doyle sniffed the leaf. His eyes cut in their direction. Instead of a formal greeting, he asked, "Do you own a cat?"

Apprehension making her skin feel too tight, Allison nodded. "A hairless, named Rabbit. He's an indoor cat."

Doyle lifted an eyebrow, eyeing first Allie, then Dee, and finally Kansas. "Couldn't have been the dog. The spray is too high and distinctly feline and male."

She felt like clapping to mock his distinguished detective skills but felt too creeped out that he was sniffing their plants and could tell the difference between cat and dog urine.

"Thanks, I think?" Dee replied.

The detective seemed too lost in thought to notice. Finally, he said, "Did you know that highly intelligent cats can be trained to climb heights to infiltrate cracks too small for a human and open windows and doors from the inside?"

"Gives a whole new meaning to the word cat burglar."

"Was there cat urine near the crime scenes?" Dee asked, catching on to something she had not.

"Perhaps."

She'd lost so much. He would *not* take her cat from her. "Rabbit doesn't go outdoors and doesn't spray. I have records of his neutering."

"Mind if I have someone collect a sample to prove this?"

Allie reared her head and wrinkled her nose. "Gross, but okay."

Detective Doyle bobbed his head. "I appreciate the cooperation. I have two more questions. Firstly, have you seen Thorne's Himalayan? The cat is missing, and we now suspect the Thornes have an accomplice using the cat."

Frustrated that the great detective was going down the wrong road again, Allie threw up her hands. "Cats? You're blaming cats!"

Kansas barked as if he agreed with her.

"There is precedence. Many criminals have had animal accomplices."

"While you're playing reverse Scooby Doo, more kids are falling victim. You need to look harder. Didn't you all get an—"

Dee grabbed her arm, digging her short nails into her skin. The pain in her flesh took her out of her rage and back into her head. She swallowed down the words "anonymous call," opting for, "Didn't you get any other leads? Cat accomplices seem so ... I don't know. Farfetched."

Indignation swept over Doyle's features. It seemed no one had ever called His Brilliance's ideas farfetched before. "I am nothing if not thorough. I'll send the forensic team to collect the urine sample."

Dread crystalized into icy shards in Allie's chest, cooling all anger. He wasn't trying to prove it wasn't the Thornes' Himalayan, he was still trying to pin the case on her and Dee.

Coming to the same conclusion, Dee stepped forward. It was her turn to be angry. "You still think we are part of this, don't you?"

"You are tied to the Thornes and the victims, so yes, I have not ruled you out as suspects. Good afternoon, ladies." With a leaf in his hand, the detective left.

Chapter Eighteen

THE LOST BOYS

*D*ee was not one for procrastination. Whatever allowed some people to fully put off responsibility until the last minute had not been installed in her. Her schoolwork had always been completed before the deadline, she filed taxes as soon as she had all the forms, she paid bills as soon as she could, immediately if it was possible. She wished it was possible to relax enough to let things go, but she hadn't. She couldn't. Not since she was eight years old and a tornado took everything from her. She did not have control over the weather that day or control over what happened in the days after. When she emerged from that cellar, she was a changed girl who was meticulously, obsessively in control.

Yet, she'd been procrastinating calling her aunt since the morning after the initial arrest. She'd sent a couple texts every day, but the thought of having to speak to her aunt and uncle was almost as unbearable as having to face Leander in the parking lot of the police station.

Ugh. Leander. She pushed him from her mind, staring at her phone.

She had to do this. Had to make the call, had to go to their house, pick them up, and drive them to the impound. It was all that jerk Doyle's fault. He let them drive to the station *and then* had the audacity to impound their car once they were inside being interrogated over nothing. Or, well, nothing as far as the police knew. Dee wouldn't be surprised if most of the residents of Snob Knob had cameras all over their properties and she was more than a little surprised the Thornes had reported their break-in. Maybe they were too embarrassed about the sex dungeon? Dee knew she was embarrassed enough for all of them.

The Prius, though, had to be retrieved and she had to have her aunt and uncle to get it. The longer it sat there, the more they would have to pay. Dee could suck up her dread of talking to Aunt Sal in order to save a couple hundred dollars.

"Dorseigh Marie, where have you been?" Aunt Sal shouted when she opened the front door. In the end, Dee decided it would be easier to drive over. The conversation wasn't going to be terrible enough over the phone, but at least she would have better luck trying to calm them both down if she was there with them instead of a voice on the phone. "I haven't slept in days! Not since the police started making those ridiculous accusations. How anyone could think you would be involved with those abductions is beyond me."

Uncle Hank was just getting to his feet from the recliner when they stepped into the living room. He surveyed her up and down and then, with a wink, asked, "How was the pokey?"

"Hank," Aunt Sal snapped. "Be serious. How do you think it was? Look at her? She's pale, and she looks like she's lost weight. Have you lost weight?"

Dee didn't think she had, but then she wasn't one to keep track. Her obsessive control did not encompass eating, thankfully.

"Ah, Sal, she knows I'm teasing." He grabbed Dee into a hug, the sweatshirt he wore slightly stale with the smell of old man sweat. She had to get back over to make sure their washer was clean and that they had better laundry detergent. One more thing for the list.

The rest of the conversation went mostly the way all her conversations with her aunt and uncle went. She promised to call more often after the situation was resolved. She promised to come to dinner more, to help with the yard and the house upkeep. She swore she would return to her normal self and take up her regular weekly activities as soon as she could. Her aunt and uncle made weak protests that she shouldn't have to take care of them, when all three of them knew she did. In fact, she ordered groceries and paid for them with her quickly dwindling resources before she got around to telling them the true purpose of her visit. At least she knew they would have food. Even with the car returned, they rarely left their home. The older they got, the less they wanted to do. It was like without her to take care of, they no longer had a purpose.

She added 'Finding senior activities' to the list.

"So," she took a deep breath. "I need your help."

In the end, it wasn't too annoying. They had to drive to the only car impound in town that was tucked behind the only industrial park in town, which consisted of one warehouse and a factory that had a full parking lot, but absolutely no indication what they were making inside the building. A stone-faced front-desk attendant ignored them for a solid ten minutes, where Dee silently and repeatedly pleaded with her aunt and uncle for patience, before the woman finally asked what she could do for them.

Five hundred gut-churning dollars and another twenty minutes later, her aunt and uncle had the Prius, and Dee made endless promises to see them as soon as she could get away. They didn't know the status of her business, and she'd never tell. As far as they were aware, she was still working, still thriving despite being suspected of kidnapping.

She returned home to find Allie sitting at her desk, listlessly reading social media.

"Punishing yourself?" Dee asked, flopping on the bed behind her roommate.

Allie closed the browser window. "Shopping. Adding all the things I sold into a shopping cart and then pretending I could afford to buy it all back."

"I'm so sorry, Allie. I shouldn't have let you do that." Especially considering Susan Glenda was such a dead end.

"No. It's fine. I'll get it all back some day. She spun in her chair, facing Dee. "So what now? Should we drive by Lee's? Maybe he's ready to talk."

Dee's stomach dropped at the sound of his name. She had to get over this. Before, she was fidgety and weird whenever she was around him or thought of him, but now she was bordering on pathetic. She didn't want to rely on him, because she did not know if she could. Not after what had happened the night before. She remembered with definitive clarity asking him what was going on, but did *not* remember him ever giving her an answer. "No. I don't want to talk to him." Almost on cue, her phone rang, Leander's name popping up. She silenced the call and squared her shoulders. It *was* time for answers, but not from either of the two men currently in their lives. They couldn't be trusted. Not right now. "I think we should go back to that cabin. *Something* kept us out and I want to know what it was."

It took nearly an hour to park and find the cabin again. Every time Dee swore they were going the right way, it felt like they were shoved back. Like a wall of negativity sprang up in their path whenever that path drew them closer to the cabin. Before being accused of crimes they hadn't committed, Dee would have said she didn't believe in the supernatural. But, times changed. She was at the point where she could believe almost anything, even magic. All things considered, she thought she was handling at least the weirdness of the situation relatively well.

Finally, after walking in circles, they either outran the bad vibes or found a way around it, because when they pushed through a wall of trees, the cabin was there, sitting innocently where they'd left it.

"Holy shit," Allie gasped. "Is that—"

They ducked back behind the trees, peeking around a trunk just enough to watch Leckermaul appear on the path the group had taken the day before. It *was* Leckermaul, Dee knew it was and yet...

"That's more than plastic surgery," Allie hissed. "That's more like her skincare routine is bathing in the blood of virgins."

"It's not just skincare," Dee hissed back. "Does virgin blood do all that?"

Leckermaul was thinner, stood taller, with a thick, dark braid that hung to her waist, and firm, high, and extremely perky breasts. She was glamorous, like a Hollywood pin-up when just two weeks before, she had been a plump, white-haired granny-type. That change wasn't possible. No one, no matter how wealthy or determined, could pull off the complete age reversal Leckermaul had seemingly achieved. At best, the celebrities who tried to pull off extensive plastic surgery ended up looking like slightly bloated felines. Even then, skin still sagged, the body unable to hold the same shape it had in youth.

"Did she find the fountain of youth?" Allie gasped as another figure appeared on the path. "Oh, no! Oh, *no*."

Dread crept up Dee's spine.

Reuben, in his unblinking, slack-jawed zombie state, followed Leckermaul. In his arms, he carried a limp child. Words floated through her mind like a distant memory *clawing at some poor half-awake kid's window*. When had she heard them? Who had said them?

She shook her head, something she seemed to be doing a lot recently. This was it, this was where they cleared themselves. They would save that kid and themselves at the same time. This entire nightmare would be over before the end of the day. She could see it all playing out; the police hauling Leckermaul (and Reuben?) away, the children all being reunited with their parents, and she and Allie heralded as heroes, their lives and clients returned.

Across the clearing, Leckermaul bent and picked up one perfectly smooth stone, walked ten steps and picked up another. She said something to Reuben before crossing the invisible border.

Dee stepped around the tree, a shout on her lips. It was time to end whatever terrible game Leckermaul was playing.

Suddenly, Dee was falling into the tall, wet grass, a weight crashing into and landing on top of her.

"What are you doing?" Allie whisper-yelled. "Do you want to be caught?"

"They have a kid." She rolled out from under Allie. "We have to do something!"

"We don't know what she's capable of, Dorseigh! We can't just start yelling at her. What do you think she's going to do? Say, 'Oh, you got me!' and then turn herself in? What if she turns us into zombies like Reuben? Being a zombie is not on the list of things I want to do with my life!"

"We can't do nothing," Dee cried softly. "We have to help."

"We will. Of course we will."

The door to the cabin slammed closed, causing Dee to nearly cry in earnest for the missed opportunity.

"She will leave, Dee. She's not going to stay inside forever. And when she does, we'll get inside. We have the key."

"She moved the stones," Dee said, glancing at the cabin over her shoulder. "Did you see that? She moved two stones and then she was able to get to the cabin."

"Yeah. Weird. Like a," Allie snapped her fingers a few times. "A whatsit called?"

"A forcefield thing." She pounded her head, trying to think of the word. "Like a witch in a storybook. I can't think of what it's called. It's right on the tip of my stupid tongue."

"Yes, exactly. Not the part about your tongue being stupid." She pointed at Dee. "She's definitely very storybook witchy."

"Storybook witches aren't real."

"Ha. Yeah, right. Tell that to those kids. Tell that to Reuben. Tell that to Mrs. Leckermaul and her long, flowing hair. Tell that to the ward that kept us out of that cabin yesterday."

Maybe Dee would. Maybe she would march right into the bakery tomorrow morning and tell Mrs. Leckermaul she knew exactly what she was.

Tomorrow, because today they waited in the weeds and the trees for Leckermaul and Reuben to leave the cabin. Alone, hopefully. If they could get to that kid, they could get the kid to the police. They could still be cleared by the end of the day.

Dee's stomach rumbled, her mouth dry. They waited, crouched outside the magical barrier for what felt like hours, but according to her watch was only about forty-five minutes. When Leckermaul and Reuben finally stepped out of the cabin, the surge of adrenaline that hit her system knocked all thoughts of food or water clear from her head. They were leaving! And she and Allie could get into the cabin.

Once the duo was out of sight, Allie placed her arm on Dee's shoulder, pressing her lips to Dee's ear. "Let's give it a few more minutes, just to make sure they're gone."

Dee swore those five extra minutes were actually longer than the prior forty-five. Her heart pounded so hard she was panting. Every second made her feel like she was going to crawl out of her own skin. She needed to get to that kid. She *had* to get to him.

Finally, Allie determined it was okay to move. Still, they crept across the open space annoyingly slowly, looking over their shoulders as they went. Both of them kicked aside stones, opening a path wide enough to drive a car through. Dee was going to throw the stones into the weeds once they were finished inside. Mrs. Leckermaul would never be able to rebuild her forcefield thingy if Dee had her way. Not that she knew what that took or how to make whatever it was called in the first place, but that didn't matter. The stones were getting tossed and that was that.

Allie dug the key out of her pocket, neither of them surprised when it slid into the old-fashioned lock and turned with ease.

Allie gave Dee a look, Dee nodded, and they pushed open the door.

Inside what should have been a perfectly boring little cabin, with a tiny kitchen to the left of the small foyer that opened to a living room/bedroom combo, was a horror show. Cages, stacked two high, lined the living room walls, a two-seater couch, a coffee table, and a twin sized bed were shoved into a corner, giving space to what looked like an operating room bed with straps to keep a patient in place and an IV hook to keep them alive. In the cages were kids, most of them empty, thankfully, with four occupied. All boys. All unconscious.

"Let's get them out." Allie stepped to the closest one, the one with the boy they had just seen brought in. But even though they were shut with standard slide locks, she couldn't budge it. "Try one of the others," she grunted, her fingers slipping on the metal.

Dee scrambled around her friend, going for the next closest occupied cage. The lock wouldn't move, not even a little wiggle. "What the fuck," she grunted, shocking herself with the curse before moving to the next cage. That one wouldn't open either, nor the last one. "They have to open. There's no reason for them to *not open*." She smacked the lock. "They should open!"

"Look around. Maybe there's something we can use."

But there wasn't anything. No tools or keys, nothing that would help them get to the kids.

"Shit. Shit, shit, shit." Allie kicked a wall. "We can't just leave them here."

"Maybe we do. Maybe we leave them and go directly to the police. Look," she dug in her bag until she found her phone. "We take pictures, and we show the police. They'll have to believe us. They'll have to come."

"Yeah. That's good. Okay, let's get pictures and get to Bertha."

They each took several showing the cages and the table as well as pictures of the outside of the cabin. Dee promised the unconscious boys they would be back with help, and they would get them out of the cabin no matter what.

She chucked five stones into the woods and shoved another into her bag.

The problem with magic, they found out, is that it doesn't play nicely. Things that should work, don't and things that should be impossible aren't. Or, in the case of the pictures on their phones, what showed clear images before (Dee knew they did, because she'd checked before leaving the cabin), were only blurred and incomprehensible smudges.

"What am I looking at here, girls?" Doyle asked, rotating Dee's phone.

"Kids," Dee answered weakly. "Pictures of kids."

"The missing kids. In cages." Allie swiped through her own photos. "We found them in a cabin in the woods, but we couldn't open the cages."

"And whose cabin were the kids in?" Doyle handed Dee back her stupid, useless phone.

"I don't know, but we saw Leckermaul–"

"Mrs. Leckermaul? The little old lady who owns the bakery?" Doyle rubbed his eyes.

"Yes, dammit. We saw her bringing in a new kid. We *saw it*."

"You saw Mrs. Leckermaul, an elderly woman, carrying a child through the woods?"

"We can show you!" Dee yelled. "We found the kids, why are we wasting time here?"

"Girls," Doyle stood. "Go home. Stop trying to help. You are not the detectives here. You are the suspects. Go home and stay there. For your own good and for mine."

"At least we didn't get arrested," Allie fumed as they slunk out of the station.

"Yeah," Dee sighed, defeated. Of course it wouldn't work out so easily. Nothing could ever work out easily. "Should we go back?"

"I don't know, but let's get out of here. I'm starving and so are our pets, I bet. These assholes are nothing but incompetent."

Dee was both starving and sick to her stomach. She'd promised those boys, and she *always* kept her promises. They would find a way to get them, though, because this was one promise she would not break.

Chapter Nineteen

DESIGNER DIVINATION

ury flared in Allie's chest, bright and hot. Her eyes stung, but she refused to release a single tear. The palpable fear behind rage so closely behind. She couldn't wipe the image of the children's ashen skin, their shallow breaths out of her mind. Leckermaul was keeping those kids in cages—*Cages!*—and that idiot Detective Doyle believed she and Dorseigh Marie McHale, the goodiest two-shoes of all goody two-shoes, were the culprits. The incompetence and laziness sent her into another rage-filled spiral. Since she couldn't set the building on fire with her glare, she tore her gaze from the police station and thrust it on her friend.

"Why would *we* hurt kids? What the Hell does he think our motive might be? They are our clients' children. How are we supposed to benefit from kidnapping them? It doesn't make sense." She loosened her grip on the steering wheel to throw up her hands. "None of this makes sense."

Dee nodded, her gaze distant. The sight of the kids must be on her mind, no doubt.

The cottage was like something out of a horror movie. Thinking about horror movies, an idea occurred to her. "Do you think Leckermaul is a vampire?"

Scrunching her face, she asked, "What?"

She tapped her temple. "Think about it. The victims aren't dead, just ... um ... mostly dead. Maybe she's like Dracula, draining them of blood and has Reuben in her thrall like Big D had Renfield."

Dee pursed her lips as if considering the outlandish proposition. "If she were draining them of blood, why not go for adults? They have more blood volume or whatever you call it. Also, the vampire theory doesn't explain the rocks. I don't know much about the occult, but I do know that I read a fantasy novel where they used rock, bone, and blood to create magical wards. Oh! I remembered!"

"Wards?"

"The magical force fields."

Allie blew out her breath. She'd heard of wards while playing fantasy games–God! She missed gaming!–but didn't think she'd ever talk about them in real life. But that's what they had done. They'd broken the ward by moving the rocks. An idea occurred to her. "If she can do that and mind control Reuben, maybe Leckermaul is a witch or a sorceress. Would it be far-fetched to believe she has the detective under her spell as well?"

Dee's shoulders slumped. "If she can put people under her spell, we need to be careful. She dumped that kid next to our dumpster."

Cold sprouted in Allie's gut. If magic was real, Leckermaul was out to get them. "You're right. She might have wanted to throw the police off by making us a mackerel."

"You mean a red herring."

"Yeah. I knew it was some sort of fish." Allie waved off the correction to get to the point. "Anyway ... as soon as the former crone gets whatever she wants out of the kids, the next logical step would be getting us to entrap ourselves."

"Judging by the looks of her earlier, she's stealing their youth. We're already in danger."

"So, we might as well be the ones to set the kids free. Do we have bolt cutters?"

"Yeah, but we need some sort of protection from her. What if she catches us as we're transporting kids out?"

Dee had a point. Allie started up Bertha and put the old girl in gear. "Let's get ourselves some protection."

～

*D*ee leaned over her shoulder, both focused on the search results on the monitor. There were plenty of online psychics, tarot, and divination experts. Some scammy looking curse breakers, too, but nobody in town. Allie didn't trust anyone she couldn't meet in real life. Too many bots and con artists online that not only wanted what you agreed to pay but access to all your personal information to steal your identity and milk everyone in your contact list.

"Try that one." Dee reached a hand in her line of vision. A single finger pointed to a listing for a shop called, "Counting Crones".

Allie sighed and opened the website. The shop sold incense, healing crystals, tarot decks, ethically sourced sage, wards against the evil eye, and various other things one would associate with some new age store.

"D'ya think she's a legit witch?"

"I don't know what to think anymore," Allie replied with a shrug. "Says here that she does tarot readings, futhark runes readings, past life regression, and—uh—tass-ee-oh-graphy."

"Tasseography?" Dee's nose wrinkled. "Sounds like nonsense to me."

Allie grinned at the judgment in Dee's tone.

"Why are you looking at me like I said something country?"

"Not country ... but you do sound like your aunt. Next, you'll gripe about the price of bread now compared to when you were a girl."

Her friend and business partner were so kind to everyone, sometimes Allie forgot she was talking to a no-nonsense midwesterner, who scoffed at her income from live-streaming fantasy games. Dee wasn't completely a troglodyte. She owned a cell phone and uploaded receipts digitally for the bookkeeping of their business, but Allie did the actual bookkeeping on the software. Dee was all nuts, bolts, paint cans and rollers, and fix-it with tools kind of thinker. She might be the only millennial that Allie knew who didn't have a personal social media. Of course, Dorseigh had her hands on her hips and her lips pinched like a church lady judging someone who came to service only at Christmas and Easter.

"Actually, that face is exactly like your aunt."

"Don't make fun of me." Dee gestured to the monitor. "That's ridiculous."

She sobered. "So is Leander and Reuben scaling buildings like Spiderman, and Leckermaul going from an old lady to looking our age." She didn't add Leckermaul's method of rejuvenation. Neither of them needed to be reminded who they were doing this for. The images of the kids' ashen faces were seared in her skull.

As if reading Allie's sober expression for what it meant, Dee relented. "Fair."

~

"Counting Crones" didn't scream storefront psychic. Actually, it didn't seem very crone-like either–Black Forest Bakery had more of that vibe. Allie thought the place would at least have a more hippie dippy, crunchy, or cottage core aesthetic, but the stylized black and white sign, the stunning landscape with exotic flowers and a water feature spoke of a high-end boutique or spa.

Inside, the place was immaculate. Glass display cases featured crystals for your every need, idols to worship, tarot and oracle cards in gorgeous boxes with gold foiling. Leather bound books lined a bookcase. Racks of essential oils, tinctures, ground powders featured the kind of bottles one would expect in an expensive perfumery. Jewelry with esoteric symbols in the display cases possessed quality craftsmanship of an artisan, and didn't appear to be cheap nickel or plastic bought in bulk from some discount online store. Dried herbs tied with pastel ribbons sat in wicker baskets, not a single leaf or twig out of place.

"I'm afraid to touch anything," Dee confided in a whisper behind her hand. Her other hand touched her chest.

Even though she'd grown up in a mansion on Snob Knob, Allie felt the same. In fact, the pristine shop made her pulse spike. A lifetime of scoldings to not touch this precious antique or that ancient vase from the blah, blah dynasty resurfaced to the forefront of her mind. "Mm-hmm. Me, too."

Part of her just wanted to leave, but those kids in cages...

The Jills of All Trades both turned to the click of heels warning them of someone's approaching presence. The woman that the heels belonged to, wore her shiny jet hair in a sophisticated chignon. Her expertly lined eyes matched a pair of emerald stud earrings and an emerald pendant on a gold chain, and she had on a classic Chanel dress with green piping so dark it was barely lighter than the bulk of the black material. Black gloves with silk bows, the same color as the suit's piping, covered her hands. Interesting that she and Susan Glenda both loved Chanel. At least the lawyer had a reason to dress this way.

This woman owned a shop, but her aura screamed, "This is very expensive. Go away."

Allie had seen the same sophistication her entire life. Her own mother dressed as such. However, her mouth dropped the same as Dee's. While her friend's eyes were wide with wonder, Allie was filled with surprise as her gaze fell to the stranger's feet—where she saw the very same diamond studded heels, she'd sold to make ends meet. This psychic overpaid for the shoes, but that's not what surprised her.

This town had too many coincidences.

As the woman gave them both a similar once over as they'd given her, Allie's skin crawled as if the gaze had a texture. Also, it was disturbing as heck, that the elegant head didn't move as her eyes surveyed them.

Dee inhaled sharply as if preparing to speak.

The shop owner held up a finger, silencing Dee and then spoke, "It's about time you came to the right witch for help. I've been waiting for you." She flashed a smile as bright as her shoes. "Follow me to the divination room."

Within ten minutes, the three were in the back of the shop seated at a round table. Although it erred more on the side of a Victorian parlor, the decor was no less expensive and tasteful as the front. Even the crystal ball at the center of a high thread count tablecloth seemed made of real crystal, perhaps a Swarovski, and the ornate stand it sat upon was polished silver.

"So, you want to know who the real kidnapper is to clear your name, don't you?" the woman who introduced herself as Zephyr asked. She circled a gloved finger over the crystal ball. "I can help, but it will cost you."

Noticing her friend was extremely uncomfortable with anything woo woo, Allie spoke up first, waving her hands. "We know who did it."

"I see." Zephyr's neutral expression flashed briefly with rage. Why would she be angry? Whatever the witch felt beyond her cool tone had disappeared as fast as it showed up. Perhaps Allison was so stressed that she'd imagined something nefarious, and all the shop owner felt was surprise. "Did you go to the police?"

Both of them slumped in their chairs. Allie sighed. "Yeah. They don't believe us."

A corner of her red lipstick painted mouth curled upward. Reclining in her seat, Zephyr waved a black-gloved hand in a circular motion. "What, then, do you need from me?"

Allie and Dee exchanged glances. Dee nodded. Might as well give it a shot. "We need a protection spell."

Her eyebrows raised a fraction. "Protection from what, pretties?"

In for a penny... "We have reason to believe that the kidnapper is a witch with mind control powers."

Allie's stomach knotted, fearing she sounded as ludicrous as when she told the police long ago that a cat had attacked her assailant, but this lady sold crystals and other witchcraft stuff. She was no cop needing hard evidence. She *had* to believe them.

"Mind control is not really in a witch's power. Most Wiccans—"

Dee finally spoke up. "She's not a Wiccan! The witch has a man under her thrall doing her bidding, and she's sucking something out of those kids that puts them in a coma and makes her look younger."

At first, Zephyr stared blankly at them. Her gaze flicked to the door. *No, no, no. She couldn't kick them out!* When her gaze returned, it fell to Allison's middle. The witch's entire countenance changed. Instead of a bored and aloof socialite, keen intelligence sparked in her eyes. "Where did you get that?"

The charm on her bracelet warmed where it touched her skin. She forced herself to not cover it even though every instinct in her screamed to hide her charm and run. "Hmm?"

"That shoe charm is *mine*."

At first, Allison was taken aback that the witch saw the same thing as Dee had, but a covetous sort of anger slithered from deep inside.

What if it was hers? No. If she dropped it at someone's house, she could be involved in harming the kids. She didn't deserve it. She was in cahoots with Leckermaul. Allie looked to Dee. She was going to tell her roommate that they should leave.

Dee wasn't paying attention to her. She leaned forward, eyes narrowing and voice hard as the diamonds on the witch's shoes as she spoke, "If you want the shoe charm, give us protection from magical influence."

Allie and Zephyr's gazes snapped to Dorseigh. Allie gaped in horror. Zephyr's features shifted as if she were open to bargaining. That's exactly what Dee intended to do. The former farm girl had on the bargaining face she used to haggle with clients for more pay. There was no changing her mind.

"How can we even trust she can make us a protection spell?" Allie spat.

"Look, the police will take the charm anyway if we don't prove our innocence."

Part of her wanted to argue that she could swallow it again. The problem was she didn't want to go to prison or leave those kids there. Also, a teeny tiny part of her didn't want Leckermaul to keep Reuben under her thrall. The thought of someone controlling him rankled. She'd tuck away why she felt protective of him at all later.

"I don't have a spell, but I have an object of great power. It keeps me from being swindled. I cannot guarantee it will work against enthrallment magic. That's something I don't work in. It's most likely she's drugging the person with herbs, but if she is using a spell to influence another person, I do have protection."

Zephyr rose and opened a side table drawer. From it, she withdrew a necklace with a small bronze key. She stroked the key. It looked similar but not identical to the one they'd found in Thorne's house. The charm on Allie's arm vibrated as if calling out for the key.

The coincidence was too great. Could Thorne also be a witch?

Dee reached out her hand to accept the key, but Allison stayed it. She wasn't sure she wanted to touch the thing. Her friend scowled, but Allie didn't care. Didn't matter. Zephyr didn't put the key within their reach anyway.

"How do we know you're not just giving us a dud and you get the real deal?"

She wouldn't need protection against Leckermaul after the police had her in custody, but she would need the *rabbit* charm. There was no doubt in her mind that if everyone saw it as a different object, it was a powerful, magically imbued charm. That made it more valuable than any short-term protection.

"I tell you what. I'm a patient woman." Zephyr smiled, revealing straight white teeth. There was something sinister about the smile that left Allie cold. "I'm so sure it will work that I will take the risk and let you *borrow* my talisman free of charge. If my magic protects you on your quest, then you will give me the charm on your bracelet and return my key. If it doesn't work, then I shall lose it and the charm."

"Why do you want it?"

She leaned forward; eyes hungrily focused on Allie's wrist. "Because any witch worth her salt will want it. That charm is everything."

Chapter Twenty

RATS IN A CAGE

he key tingled in the palm of Dee's hand, heavy and smooth, except around the intricate bow where there was a rough seam. Dee ran her middle finger over and over the seam, fixated on how it caught at her skin. She knew what she had to do, but rubbing the key was easier. She doubted it would do anything. That woman was almost certainly a charlatan, had probably only traded false hopes, a fake talisman, a sure path to their destruction.

But Leckermaul was real, and they had to have something on their side. She guessed maybe false hope was better than none.

"Are you ready?" Allie asked, steering them down Leander's street.

She wasn't. The sting of betrayal was still too strong. Which, she was self-aware enough to admit, made very little sense. Leander had gone above and beyond for her. He'd done way more than was required for their moderately-beyond-a-standard-acquaintance friendship. No matter what scenarios she'd made up, he wasn't obligated to her. He was allowed his secrets.

But, also, she was in deep shit. Allie was in deep shit. And as someone who *was* a friend, or close enough to it, he should have been spilling all the info Dee knew he had, all the things they needed to know.

"No. I'm still mad at him and I don't understand why he hasn't helped more."

Saying that out loud made her feel ungrateful. He had done a lot, but, also, he had done just barely enough.

Ugh, this sucked.

"So, let's ask him. Let's make him answer."

"How?"

Allie rolled the truck to a stop outside his house. It was a rundown clapboard, single story home with a garage sprouting from the side that was bigger than the entire house. Unlike most of the streets in Sueños, this street was mostly small houses on large lots. Their own home, while not huge, was at least twice as big as Leander's, but with a tiny front yard, only a couple feet on the sides, and a little garden in back. Dee was constantly picking up after Kansas to keep them from being buried under an avalanche of dog poop.

"What's the plan again?"

Allie rolled her shoulders, eyes narrowing, as she absently caressed the shoe charm on her bracelet. "We are marching up to his door. We are demanding answers. We are not leaving until he tells us something we can use. Something useful."

Sure. Useful. As if she knew what that would sound like. They'd just been to a person who read futures and sold spells. To her, that was about as useless as lipstick on a pig. But, there they were, holding a supposed talisman that would protect a man from outside control.

She sighed, opened the passenger door, and walked up the broken sidewalk. Lee should really take better care of his yard. Weeds sprouted in corners and cracks, spurge and chickweed taking up residence along the porch like they belonged, a half-rotted fence sagged along one side of the yard while the other side of the fence had given up completely, lying half buried in the ankle-high grass.

To her surprise, the front door opened before her foot touched the first step up to the porch.

"Hey." Lee stepped out, closing the door behind him, and stood at the top of the two steps, blocking her path. "What are you doing here?"

Well. That wasn't the response she'd been expecting. Any other time, and especially if she was here by herself, she would have mumbled an apology and ran away. But, she wasn't there alone. Allie was at her back and without even seeing her, she knew Allie was bristling.

"I think..." Her voice shook. Damnit. She cleared her throat and tried again. "We need answers. We got into the cabin. There were four little boys in there. In *cages*. They were all unconscious."

Lee closed his eyes but didn't respond.

"The cages were locked somehow, and we couldn't get them open. The cops didn't believe us. We're going back to get them–"

"No." His eyes flew up, and he stepped down one stair.

"Yes." Dee backed up, too, knocking into Allie who steadied her with a hand to the back. "We're getting those kids, and if you don't want to help, that's *fine*. We'll do it alone, but we need to know what is going on. We need to know if Leckermaul is a–"

"Witch. She's a damned witch, and we need to know what you know about it, Lee." Allie stepped around Dee, shoving a finger into Leander's chest. "Because you know something, maybe everything, but you're not telling us shit, and we are over it!"

Leander caught Allie by the shoulders. "Hey, keep your voice down." He looked over his shoulder, sending Dee into a mini panic attack.

Who was in his house? Who did he want to keep from hearing their conversation? The town might be small, but there were several women he could be hiding in there. Several tall bombshells with curves in all the right places instead of the hip dips and love handles she was cursed with.

"We need to talk," Dee said quietly, obeying his request without even realizing it. "You need to arm us with your knowledge, so we know how to deal with Leckermaul."

He sighed deeply, running both hands through his tangled hair, obviously put upon by such a request. "Fine, but inside." He held up both hands as the two moved closer to him. "You can't freak out."

Dee scoffed, a noise she never made, now certain there was a woman inside. "We can't promise that." She crossed her arms, glaring. "If you don't want us in your house, then meet us out somewhere. But, now. We need to get this conversation out of the way, because Allie and I have things to do. Saving kids is more important than whatever you have going on in there."

Allie turned her head and mouthed, *Damn.*

To Dee's shame and satisfaction, Leander flinched.

"There's nothing going on. Of course I'll help you, but don't get your hopes up. I don't know much, and whatever I do know, I've learned by mistake."

Literally the same for them. If a kid hadn't been dumped in their yard, they'd still be ignorant of the unexplainable events happening in Sueños Del Mar. He wasn't special just because he'd had more accidents than they had.

"Fine. Lead the way."

Allie reached back, lacing their hands together.

The inside of his house wasn't anything out of the ordinary, set-up mostly the same as her aunt and uncles. They walked into a small living room, tidier than the yard, but cluttered with a large gray sectional and a square coffee table. The walls were bare except for a flat screen set to one side of the front window. And, of course, the man chained to a heavy wooden dining room chair.

"What the fuck," Dee gasped and then slapped a hand over her mouth.

"Hello, ladies. Allison," Reuben purred, smiling widely despite his current state.

Allie whipped around, furious and so beautiful, Dee almost cursed again. "Get him out. Now!"

Leander's eyes flashed with something—either fear or awe—but he didn't budge. "I can't do that. It's for his own good."

"It's true," Reuben confirmed, sounding way too happy for a man chained to a chair. "If I'm here, I can't be out there—"

"Kidnapping children and taking them to Leckermaul's cabin?" Dee finished for him. "We saw you. You're *helping* her."

It wasn't fair, and she knew it, but it had to say something about his character that he was so easily manipulated.

"I wouldn't say that, exactly." His smile only dropped a little, but she figured that was because she was the one who said it. Had it been Allie, he probably would have said something flirty and nonsensical.

"How is she controlling you?" Allie asked, and sure enough his smile blazed back. "That is what's happening, right? She controls you somehow."

He shrugged, rattling the chains. "I wish I knew. One second, I am myself and in the next, I lose myself completely. I wake up sometime later with no memory of where I've been or what I've done."

It was so ridiculous.

Just like Leckermaul being a witch and the police testing for cat urine and a lawyer who turned down money to represent two clearly innocent people.

"We might have something that helps." Allie held her hand out, palm up, flicking her fingers towards Dee. "But we won't know unless Leckermaul summons you or whatever. How often does this happen?"

Reuben explained the frequency of the missing hours, focusing the summary toward Allie and only Allie. He was so obsessed with her, no one else in the room mattered. Out of his fugue state, he hadn't seen Leckermaul in her new pin-up era. Or so he said. Maybe he was equally obsessed with the new, improved Leckermaul, since he seemed to like pretty things.

Dee stole a glance at Lee, but he was staring at his feet.

Leander was not the only man in the world. There was a man who attended a booth at the weekly Farmer's Mart. He was sort of funny, a little clumsy, and tripped over his tongue whenever she asked him a question. But, he also blushed to the roots of his straw-blond hair whenever he saw her and was always attentive no matter how busy his stall. He would set aside the best ears of corn and the reddest straw-berries, pulling them out for her. Maybe she would flirt back the next time she saw him. She turned her attention back to Reuben. He apparently kept solid records of when the blackouts happened, and they seemed to align with the disappearance of the kids and even the reap-pearances. He figured he was the first to arrive at their house the night the boy was left because he came to only a block away.

The more he spoke, the angrier she became. These *boys* (because surely men wouldn't act the same) had let them take the fall and flail around when they had some knowledge of the strange events, but instead of stepping forward, had said nothing.

"Well, thanks for letting us take the fall," Dee cut in when it seemed like Allie would not. "That was mighty big of you."

"Dee," Allie sighed. "What would it have done for him to say anything?"

"What do you mean? He's actually involved in this." She stabbed her finger at him. "*He took the kids* and put one in our yard."

"We don't know that."

"No, I think we do." She looked from person to person, but none of them seemed to want to agree with her. Fine. She didn't need them to. "You know what? Forget it. I don't need to hear anymore."

"Dee!" Allie shouted, but she was already out the door.

She didn't have her keys, but she was suddenly angry enough that a walk home sounded great. She'd grab a hand saw and get those boys out no matter what. If Leckermaul tried getting in her way, she'd use the hand saw on her. She might be a witch, but Dee bet she still bled.

She heard arguing from inside the house, but didn't stop. Hopefully, they thought she needed to cool off and didn't come after her. She was getting those boys. She was tired of talking about it and not doing it.

"Hey."

Leander fell into step beside her. It took all of her restraint to not scream.

"Go away. I don't want to talk to you." She set her jaw and continued stomping away from his house with its stupid messy yard and stupid bare living room.

"Dee, come on. Come back and let's talk. I thought you wanted to talk."

Oh, fuck him for real.

She stopped. "You know, it's not exactly great thinking about how much you've kept from us this entire time. You haven't been surprised by any of this, but instead of clueing us in to anything, you've kept your secrets and let Allie and I blunder around." Her face burned, blood rushing through her face and ears. She'd never been this angry. It was refreshing and terrifying. "How dare you ask me to come back and talk now? Where were you last week?"

He opened his mouth and then closed it. "I—"

"I'm going to get those boys, and there's nothing you can do to stop me."

Which, she found out, was wrong. She took two steps before he grabbed her around the waist and then flipped her around and over his shoulder.

"What are you doing?" she shrieked.

"I'm sorry." To his credit, he did sound sorry. "But you can't go by yourself."

"Are you going to chain me to a chair too?"

"You know I'm not," he said wearily. "You know I'd never do that."

"Except, you did it to Reuben."

He set her down on the porch. "He asked me to do that. Brought his own chains and everything. They're special, I guess. They'll keep him in place even if the witch calls him."

Now it was Dee's turn to flinch. So, she was a witch. That must be the popular opinion of her, then.

"Are you going to explain anything?"

"Yes." His big hands held her shoulders. "I'll tell you what I know. Whatever will help."

Those two things weren't necessarily the same things, but she would take whatever he'd give at this point. If she still wasn't satisfied, she'd leave. But the next time, she'd demand the keys to Bertha first.

"I'm on your side, Dee." One of his hands slid from her shoulder to cup her face, tilting it up towards him. "It might not seem that way, but I am."

She pulled away from him. He'd had so many chances to be on her side, to prove that he was, but he'd waited until threatened. He could keep his proclamations until she had proof of his intent.

"Whatever. Let's get this over with."

❧

She sat on the short end of the couch, folded against the arm, head down, shoes on. She should have removed them. She never kept them on in her own house and covered them with little foot booties whenever entering a client's home, but fast getaways weren't as possible when you weren't wearing your shoes.

Allie sat on the other end, as close as possible to Reuben, still in his chains. Leander stood in the door between the living room and the dining room beyond.

"It's getting dark," Dee pointed out at the same time Allie said, "We went to see a witch."

Of course, Allie's statement got the males' attention.

"What do you mean?" Reuben snapped. "What witch?"

"She owns a shop." Allie's eyes darted to Dee and then back to Reuben. She lifted her chin, haughty and regal. "We went to see how to protect you. She gave us this." Allie pulled the key out of a pocket. "She said it is a protection against swindlers, but it may also work against enthrallment. We thought we might need something to protect us against Leckermaul ... when we go to get the kids."

"That's a horrible idea," Reuben snarled, pulling against the chains. "Do you want her to control you as well? That little bauble won't stop her."

Allie leaned forward, touching it against Reuben's bare arm.

"Oh," he sighed, relaxing. "That's nice."

Tingley, Dee wanted to add, but didn't. She sank deeper into the couch.

"I don't know how strong it is—"

"It's strong." Reuben rattled in his chains as Allie sat back.

"But it's more than what we have now. And it seems like if we want to get those boys, we're going to have to do it all ourselves. It's either that or leave town and—"

"You can't leave." Leander tracked the key with his eyes. "None of us can."

Allie scoffed. "That's ridiculous. Of course, we can leave."

"No." He shook his head. "That's, uh, where I took you the other night after," he waved his hand at Reuben. "I drove us to the town line. You crash into it, and it resets time. At least a few minutes, maybe a couple hours. I don't know how long for sure. I just know it's there, and it won't let us out."

Dee felt sick, her stomach twisting itself into a knot. She'd never tried to leave before because she never had a reason. But, she hadn't always been here. She knew that. She came with her aunt and uncle sometime during her high school years. Before that she lived... Somewhere else? Definitely somewhere else. It was right at the tip of her tongue. She shook her head. She was tired and hungry and worn out. She'd think of it later.

"People come and go all the time," Allie argued.

"Yeah, noncitizens. Those of us who live here can't leave."

"That cannot be true," Dee said from her couch corner.

"It is. I ran into it once when I was... Um, out for a jog. I ran right into it and woke up in my bed. It knocked me back to earlier in the day. You don't remember it, though, right? You don't remember running into it at all, so I did it again and same thing. Wound up in my bed, no idea how I got there."

Reuben snickered. "How many times did you slam yourself into the barrier, little lion man?"

Leander ignored him. "I've tried to leave, but every time I end up at home. We can't leave."

Allie ran out of the room, pushing past Leander. A second later, they heard water hitting the sink. It was almost loud enough to drown out Allie's semi-hysterical shriek.

In some odd way, it felt right, knowing they were trapped.

"Why didn't you just tell us that the other night? Instead of crashing into the barrier? You could have told us what to expect."

"I know. I'm sorry. I didn't think you'd believe me."

She ignored him. "To the best of our understanding, Leckermaul placed wards around the cabin. Maybe it's the same with the town. Maybe someone stronger than her has us trapped here."

Reuben shivered, rattling his chains.

From behind Leander, Allie asked, "What do we do now?"

Dee didn't know if all four of them would want to be a part of the plan. Her and Allie, sure, but the other two needed to commit or get out.

"Are you two in?" Dee asked them, an imposter speaking with her voice. She didn't make rescue plans. She was not a hero. But she was going to do this and didn't need dead weight with her. "We're going to use the key from Zephyr and we're going to get those boys. We just need to know who is with us and when to go."

"I am, Dee. You know I want to help," Leander said solemnly. And it sucked, because she wished she could go back to him being a guy she sometimes took her truck to who was kind of a good-natured airhead and not this solemn, but wishy-washy man.

"Count me in," Reuben said smiling. "I would like to not spend the next significant period of my life chained to a chair."

So, that was it. The four of them and a probably false talisman against some sort of life force-sucking witch.

No problem.

Chapter Twenty-One

HEART-SHAPED BOX OF THE FOREST

The cottage seemed uncannily still, like a predator waiting in ambush. Instead of tall grass, pretty gardens blended with a cozy exterior—a camouflage to lull prey into a false sense of security. A story from her childhood surfaced from the recesses of her mind; an image of a candy laden cottage from a picture book. Another picture-memory emerged of a witch shoving children fattened by the candy exterior into an oven.

Allie shook her head. The parallel of the formerly old woman draining the kids of their youth and literally consuming them was too much. A shiver of fear slithered down her back. Were they really going to face a witch with that kind of power with nothing but an antique-looking key?

"This victory will be for the people. No more monarchs. No more tyranny," Allison murmured. She crouched low, holding bolt cutters like a weapon. One good hit to the back of the head would knock an unsuspecting witch out.

Reuben, on Allie's left, whispered, "Aye, Wandergirl."

Dorseigh and Leander flanked her right. Dee held a pair of bolt cutters, and Leander kept a handsaw hanging from his toolbelt. The wholesome features of Dee's girl-next-door pretty face hardened with resolve. Lee looked like he swallowed a fly—nothing about the big guy seemed at ease.

Ignoring Leander, Allie let Dee's resolve bolster her own wavering determination. She closed her eyes and inhaled. She'd faced battles before where she was outnumbered and outgunned. Virtual battles, but when she played, they *felt* real.

She eyed Reuben. Unlike the other two, Reuben seemed at ease, as if they were hanging out. As if he'd broken into witch's houses on the regular. His mouth held its usual too bright grin, and his eyes danced with mirth. Something preternatural and old lurked behind those young eyes.

How had she been duped into believing he was just a nobody? Reuben wasn't just some dude. Men with a jawline and an intellect like his didn't end up working in a bakery either. He had layers, and if she peeled them back, a past she might not want to know would be at the center.. Why else would he be in Sueños Del Mar, and why else would a witch pick him as an assistant?

The handsome and mysterious man was something more than human, too. *What* he was, and Leander for that matter, would remain to be seen. Right now, she was glad she had them here. She and Dee could handle themselves, but they were up against a supernatural power. Fighting fire with fire worked best.

Dee nodded to Leander and whispered, "You're up."

The big man crouched low and took off in a sprint too fast for Allie's eyes to track. She glanced at her friend. Dorseigh's eyes widened for a brief second before she met her gaze. Allie lifted her eyebrows in a silent, *"See why I wanted them to come?"* Her roommate grimaced but finally relented with a nod, admitting that yes, Allie was right.

Well, there was one victory tonight.

Leander held up a hand and then stepped forward. When nothing happened, that was their signal that he'd broken the ward.

"Your turn," Allie mouthed to Reuben.

He sprang into action, making a sweep around the house while Leander stood guard. Satisfied, he signaled that all was clear.

The witch wasn't inside. Good. A modicum of the heaviness that had settled in her chest lifted. Not that it was much of a relief. Every sinew of muscle in her body still coiled tight with tension.

Reuben reached into a flowerpot and produced a key, unlocking the door. He held it open and made a sweeping gesture for Allison to go in. Dee gave him a suspicious glance but went in first. Allie followed into the dark cottage. The scent of incense and herbs hit her nostrils right away. It was close to that of the Counting Crones. Unlike the soft melody playing in the divination shop, the kids' shallow breaths filled the room. At least they were breathing. The boy that had been found by her garbage bins was still in a coma, too.

A dark thought occurred. What if they got the kids out but what the witch had done to them was irreversible? She'd put a lot of faith in someone she'd found on the internet and who made money selling rocks with supposed powers and tarot readings. Unease curled in her stomach. Leckermaul didn't advertise that she was a witch. Allie had long known that people who bragged about their talent usually had less than those that had it in spades. Maybe Zephyr only had a little magic, and thought she could reverse the spell, but Leckermaul was more powerful? What if Zephyr's talisman's protection could be broken like a ward?

A light flickered on. Her fears scattered with the darkness. There were kids in cages to save.

"Huh, don't know how I knew that was there," Reuben remarked, scowling at the light switch.

"Ponder it later," Dee commanded, "Let's get to work."

The four of them managed to cut and saw open the locks. All except one.

"We'll work on this lock while you two take the others to the truck."

Reuben took the talisman on a chain off his neck. The backs of his fingers lightly brushed her cheek as he hung the long chain on Allie. Their eyes met. Butterflies stirred in her gut. She immediately stomped them out. There was no time for whatever that response meant.

His grin seemed to say he knew what his touch did to her. It fell away for a more solemn expression. He tapped the key hanging just above the swell of her breasts. "In case the witch comes back."

Leander and Reuben ran the kids in fireman's carry out the door. Knowing they'd run faster than she could, Allie concentrated on the lock. The new kid looked less sickly than the others and hadn't been there the last time she'd come.

"If Reuben's been with Leander, who did she use?" Dee asked.

Before Allie could even form a reply, a heavy thud behind them made the two spin around. An unconscious preteen girl with curly hair sprawled on the floor in a disheveled heap at Leckermaul's booted feet. The witch wore all black and her lips were painted a dark shade of crimson. Her skin appeared fresh and dewy, none of her looked more than sixteen years old.

"I'm strong enough now to do my own dirty work." Her German accent was still thick, but the voice had less of the throaty rasp of an elderly woman and more of the bright soprano of a woman younger than Dorseigh and Allison. The witch smiled, revealing white, straight teeth. Her pale blue eyes scanned the empty cages, then flinted darkly. "What did you do with the children?"

"They're going home," Allie spat, angry that Leckermaul had the nerve to sound concerned for the kids after draining them and keeping them in cages.

She arched an eyebrow. "Are they now?"

Allie and her friend pushed to their feet at the same time, facing the witch side by side. She didn't have to look to know Dee was glaring at Leckermaul, too. As she ripped the words from Allie's thoughts, Dee replied, "Yes. And, so are these two." She gestured to the girl on the floor and the boy in the cage. "And you're going to jail."

Allison had no idea how they were going to accomplish any of it, but she nodded along as if they had it all figured out.

Leckermaul cackled, loud and without mirth—the sound uncanny coming from a teenager's lips. "Haven't you figured it out yet? We're already in a prison, ladies, and I'm your only hope of getting out." She touched her chest. She reached out her hand, palm up. "But I shall have something from you first."

The key dangling from Allison's neck ripped free, breaking the chain with a snap. Then the ostensible protective talisman flew into the witch's open hand.

"Huh. This would have worked against me before." Her crimson lips spread in a malicious grin as she looked at them from beneath her eyelashes. She held out her free hand. "But, I'm too powerful now."

The intense need to flee bubbled up inside Allison. Her gaze darted to the door. Even if she wanted to run, she couldn't. She couldn't do a damned thing. She had lost all control of her limbs, her mouth. She couldn't even freaking blink.

In the same predicament, Dee whined.

Leckermaul ignored them as she eyed the talisman. "You really need to know how to use an item of power. They're useless without knowledge of how to draw protection from them. Hmm ... this is not what I sensed. This is witchcraft, not sorcery. So basic for the amount of power the crafter possesses. She has forgotten spellwork and is mucking with limited knowledge. Good. Or else she'd have known to teach you to use it properly with your own magic. You two are brimming with it. I would have pegged you two as good witches, who remembered their power, but you wouldn't have gone about this so stupidly if you had."

Allie would have gasped at the knowledge she had magic, that she might be a witch, but all she could do was sharply inhale. Dee made an angry sound or at least tried. She, too, seemed incapable of speaking or moving.

Leckermaul flicked her fingers.

One of the cage doors swung open, clanging against itself. The girl on the floor levitated, her head and body seemed fully supported as she floated into the cage. The door slammed shut. A lock flew out of a kitchen cupboard and slapped onto the cage.

"I have two options," Leckermaul began as she made a fist and lifted it.

Allie felt weightless yet cushioned. Her stomach flipped as she spun from upright to horizontal. Her body floated parallel to Dee's over to the kitchen table, landing gently atop the wood surface. Only able to move her eyes, she could see Dee was next to her.

"One is to cut out hearts and eat them. That's the old way of sourcing magic from a person in *our* realm. However, I find it messy. I stopped eating people ages ago." Leckermaul told them with as much emotion as if she'd been talking about a fad diet.

Despite being sickened by the casual mention of cannibalism, Allie wanted to make a quip about monologuing and it not working out for villains. She had to hold out hope Reuben or Leander would save the day.

Leckermaul stood next to Dee. Only a crease between her eyebrows marred her flawless skin. "Don't judge. I only did it to protect myself. When a woman has power, she can live in the woods alone and not be bothered by the designs of men. Even in this realm, before I came to remember who and what I am, I chose to be away from the society they created. I had no idea, but my instinct to survive was great."

Allie could hardly pay attention. She knew something terrible was coming. However, if she did get out of this alive, she needed to know *why* Leckermaul did it to prove her own innocence and also to discover what the witch meant by them already being in prison.

Leckermaul put a hand over Dee's chest. As it glowed with a soft amber light and the witch's hand sucked that light out, Dorseigh groaned in agony.

No, no, no! She couldn't lose Dee!

Allie screamed for the witch to stop whatever she was doing, but nothing came out but a muted whine.

Dee stopped making sound. Her skin—her flawless, dewy skin with rosy cheeks lost all color. She was as ashen and lifeless as the kids.

Tears slid from the corners of Allie's eyes and down the side of her cheek into her ears, hot and wet.

Leckermaul moved from Dee to her, stroking her hair from her face. The tender gesture at odds with the horror she just inflicted. "Don't you ever wonder why some people come and go and others never leave? Have you intended to go on a trip, got to the edge of town, and ended up in bed with some malady that prevents you from going anywhere, but you can't quite remember how you got to bed?"

Why was the witch asking these questions? They couldn't reply and couldn't think about it after she was gone.

The door burst open, Leander with Reuben on his tail entered the fray. The big man roared and leapt. The other, out of Allie's line of vision hissed. Both froze midair. Then crashed into the wall as if tossed by a giant hand. Their bodies landed with a sickening thud.

There was nothing she could do to save herself or her friends, not to mention the innocent kids.

"Don't cry. She didn't die. She's just sleeping, like the others," Leckermaul soothed.

Allie wished she could shoot lasers from her eyes. Whatever the witch did, hurt, and she didn't know how to fix it, to bring Dee back from the magical coma.

"Honestly, I was afraid she would die. She's so much older and her Spark is tied more closely to her physical manifestation." She moved to the other side of the table, pushing back Allie's hair from her forehead with cold fingers. Her skin tingled where the witch made contact. "When I'm done, we'll all go home. Our power will be restored, and this will all be a bad dream."

She then left Allie's side to approach Leander. "Hmmm... I wouldn't have risked four adults, but *he* will notice that I've taken one of his. I realized too late, you see, that she was his and not one of mine. I must take light from all of you and then find where you've hidden his trinket. Then I will free us all from this nightmare. The risk is worth it. You'll see."

At first, she thought the witch was talking gibberish, but then Allie remembered the rabbit charm. Everyone wanted it. It had to be an object of great power. Leckermaul had said that the talisman would have worked better if she'd used it. Desperate, she decided to try to use the charm to break free of the witch's hold. Allison willed the charm to protect her, chanting in her head, *"Set me free."*

Her wrist felt warm like she'd dipped it in a circlet of warm water. Then, sensation spread to her fist and fingers. She tested wiggling them. In her periphery, she could see the light from Leander's heart being drained. At the same time, the warmth spread up her arm.

Set me free! Set me free!

She sat up in time to see Leander keel over, lifeless. No, not lifeless. Drained of whatever spark existed within them, but his big chest moved with his breaths. Not noticing Allie had sat up, the witch had moved directly over to Reuben.

On rubbery legs, Allie slid off the table. Her gaze swept the room for a weapon. She grabbed a bolt cutter from the floor. Moving as swiftly as she could in that state, she charged the witch swinging the tool. The end connected with Leckermaul's head.

Or, at least it should have. It stopped just short of doing any damage. The witch lifted her free arm. An unseen force swept the ground from under her feet. She was airborne, arms and legs pinwheeling. Pain burst up her back as she slammed into a cage. Reuben slumping against the wall was the last thing she saw before everything went black.

Chapter Twenty-Two

WITCH OF THE WOODS

The problem with being the mightiest being in an entire plane of existence is that sometimes your subjects rebel. They don't like what you've done or how the world works or some other nonsense. They begin thinking that maybe they are stronger, maybe their plans are better, maybe they should be in charge. What they don't know is that they are only a child's idea of powerful and terrible.

I should know, since I'm the one who brought them here.

I suspected it was her, right from the start. The first missing child gave it away. You can take the witch out of the forest, even make her forget who and what she was, but she will still find herself in a cabin, consuming the life of the helpless.

The charm, though, is something new. I would bet all my remaining magic she didn't have it in her possession until tonight. The girls have had it, and even though I want it back—need it back—it was safe enough with them. They aren't awake enough to know what to do with it. Eventually, I would have had it back in my hands.

Now, however, I must retrieve it immediately. The witch has it. She's figured out just enough to make a mess of things. I should have

stopped her before. But after all these years, I have grown too compla-
cent. I have been watching while they age and forget the why and how
of their former lives.

I cannot be a passive watcher any longer.

Another blast of power ripples over the town, setting my teeth on
edge. There is no more time. I must get to them—to *her*—faster than
my feet will take me. Faster than my feet will take me anywhere.

If I could change anything, I wouldn't have chosen this old body to
host my spirit.

I reach out to that fool, Doyle, touching his mind with urgency. He
is asleep, nodding off at his desk after hours and days and weeks of
banging his head against the mystery of the missing children. In only a
matter of minutes, I will help him solve his mystery. I speak into his
mind where I stand, what I need, and it only takes him two more tran-
quility shattering blasts before he's there in the metal beasts the
humans of this world favor.

"To the western border," I tell him.

He nods, silent, a blank slate waiting for me to fill in all the empty
spaces.

Lights flicker all around us as he speeds towards our destination.
The citizens of this world I've created may not remember magic, but it
remembers them. If I do not stop the hag soon, they may begin to
wake and without the joined charms, I may not be able to stop it. My
power must be consolidated or else we will all be lost.

"Wait here. Your time will come soon."

The trek through the woods is long, long, *too long*. The witch's
growing power coalesces around me, so thick it seeps from the air into
my skin. Taking a deep breath, I suck it in. Foolish of her to let all this
magic go free. Perhaps she does not remember as much as I initially
feared.

Finally, finally, the cabin is there, just through the trees, light
blazing like an inferno through the dead silence of the surrounding
woods. Her ward is up, but weak, likely created before she had the full
knowledge of what she was doing. Inside the cabin, she shrieks when I
break it, stepping through like it was a ward of tissue.

Magic blasts me as I swing the door open. The scene inside is as I suspected it would be. The witch, young and lovey with all vitality of youth and overabundance of magic running through her veins, draining the essence from the blonde girl, the lion, the cat slumped on the ground, the other girl laid out on a kitchen table, all depleted of their magic.

"You," she snarls, full to bursting with the life force of my citizens, my people, the population I created a safe space for, that I vowed to protect.

"Witch." The concentration of magic shakes the cabin, cracks form and splinter the walls, racing across the ceiling, the foundation creaks and groans. The fool will bring the entire structure down on her head.

She drops the lion. "Did you think you could trap us here forever? Did you think we would all forget? Never remember who or what we are?"

Once, I had hoped that. It took tremendous power to bring them all here and even more to keep them. I'm not about to let all my hard work and years of providing safety go to waste. She does not need nor deserve to hear what I am or what my plans or reasons are.

"Give me the charm, Hilde. It does not belong to you."

"I will *never* give you anything, except a swift death." She takes a step my way, wobbling on ostentatiously tall shoes.

She is painfully beautiful, so full of the life of others. She has never been so before. She sprang to life as an old woman, alone in the woods, waiting for wayward children. This version of her is an abomination.

The charm calls from the blonde girl, begging to be home, demanding I channel it for its purpose. But I cannot, not with Leckermaul between us. I will not alert her to its presence. Leckermaul doesn't have it, and I will keep it that way. All this wasted magic is all I will need to defeat a storybook witch.

"You won't win this." I want to blast her away, send her to where she thinks she wants to go, but restraint is needed. She will have to take the fall for the missing children. It's not in the lines for the girls to do so. They will go back to their little lives, Leckermaul will be accountable, and Sueños Del Mar, my city of dreams, will go back to sleep.

"I don't need to win anything." The hate in her will be her undoing. "I only need to destroy you."

A surge of power rushes from her. An impressive amount, truly, considering how much drips down the crumbling walls. It might have been enough to damage, if she knew what she was doing. But she's only just begun to awake and does not yet have the control needed to destroy something she doesn't understand.

"I am sorry, Hilde." I allow the surge to hit full force, feeling the essence of all those she's stolen from. They twist and slide and search for their true owners. Closing my eyes, I whisper to each thread, to each color of life, untangling while they cry out to be reunited with their home. The witch still holds pieces, but I set free the essence she's expelled in her haste and her hate.

"What are you doing?" She screams, rushing forward.

Raising a hand, she freezes with her pointed red nails a breath from my face.

"None of this is yours, witch." A streak of steel gray races through her blonde hair, followed by small lines creasing the corners of her eyes. "You cannot keep it. It has to go back."

"No," she hisses, those bright blue eyes wide with sudden terror. "You can't. I—"

"In your story, Hilde Leckermaul, you are not all powerful. You prey on children, and I am not a child."

With her momentarily contained, I call the missing charm home. It snaps the thin link holding it to the blonde girl's bracelet, flying straight and true into my raised hand. To reach my true strength, it will need to be with the other pieces of my power, but it is enough to ensure I will defeat a half-awake witch with stolen magic.

"In this story," I say as her skin sags, her waist thickens, those full breasts wilt, and the flowing hair turns brittle, "you will be charged with kidnapping and poisoning all those children. You will take the fall for your crimes."

"No," she cries with a weakened voice as I drain all the stolen magic until she is too weak to stand, until the seams of her dress pop and rip. I am a kind master, though, and bring a dress more appropriate for her age through the ether.

"You will want to change into this, Hilde, before the authorities arrive."

I leave her on the floor, aged and fragile, stopping to touch the cat's head. Out of them all, he's a creature of higher magic, of greater awareness, and I'm going to need him to bear witness to what has happened here.

Once his Spark is returned, he blinks up at me with intelligent eyes.

"I need your help."

He nods much as Doyle had, but not blank. He has been blank enough lately. Time for him to know.

"You stopped her?" he asked, his voice raw.

"Of course. Can you stand?"

He brings all the boys from the truck back to the cabin, placing them back in the cages now locked with a human lock and full of enough essence to soon wake. Once the boys are where they need to be, he carries the girls and the lion to the truck with instructions to take everyone home, to get them in their bed, and for him to go wherever it is he lays his head at night. Once he's done those things, he's to keep the end of this night to himself. I let him see my true self, the untapped magic that lives in me, I let him know what I can do to him if he forgets what I've told him.

"I won't let you down."

He won't, of course. He's a smart boy.

By the time he's gone, Leckermaul has pulled herself to a table littered with pieces of cracked plaster and tipped cups.

"You will pay for this," she threatens, her thin hair floating around her head in a broken halo.

"I pay every day, dear woman. Not as much as you, though, I fear." Doyle's mind wakes up. "And the town, of course. Where will they get their baked goods now?"

"You can't keep us here forever. We do not belong here!"

"I am keeping you alive, you fool," I say with a sneer. "The good detective is on his way, Hilde. I'm sorry for what you will endure, but it is what you deserve."

~

A nose poked Dee on the cheek. She pushed at it with an arm as weak as a noodle.

"Kansas," she croaked, "stop."

Kansas did not stop. He poked again, followed by a series of licks and whines.

"I know, I know. Just give me a minute."

Stars above, her head ached. Was she sick? Was this the flu?

What day was it? Was there a job? She *should* get up. There was something to be done. There was always something to be done, but she couldn't seem to move, her head full of cotton. And pain. She knew it was there despite not moving. Her skin throbbed and she knew if she managed opening her eyes, she'd see bruises dotting her skin.

What had she done? If she could just clear the cotton, maybe she'd remember.

Against intense resistance, she peeled her eyelids apart, blinking the white expanse of her ceiling into focus. This was good, fine, great job. She didn't need to do anything else, right? She was suddenly certain it was a Sunday. They never scheduled anything on Sundays. So, yes, she could lie in bed all day and save finding out how much she ached until the next day. Or, even the day after.

Curiosity was a bitch, though, and after a few long minutes of staring at the ceiling, she lifted her head enough to look down her body. She was on top of her blankets wearing filthy jeans and a tattered sweatshirt.

"Hey," she bleated at no one, "I liked this sweatshirt."

With a bone-weary groan, she rolled off the bed, taking Kansas with her. Like the graceful being he was, he landed on his feet, but Dee hit the floor on her hands and knees, the impact jolting her already pounding head.

"Crap."

With care and slow movements, she finally got to her feet and stumbled down the hall to Allie's room, breathing a sigh of relief when she saw her roommate also in her bed, also lying on top of her covers in filthy clothes.

"Al," she breathed, her voice as weak as her knees. "Allie."

Allie groaned, one arm wrapped around Rabbit, who sent Dee a possessive glare.

"Coffee," Dee announced to whoever was listening.

No one answered, but Kansas danced at her feet.

She trudged downstairs one small shuffling step at a time. She added aspirin to her small mental list. Coffee and aspirin. The break-fast of champions.

Something moved in the front room wrenching a full-throated scream from Dee followed by a squeal as she lost her footing and fell down two steps.

"Dee," Allie shouted from her room.

The shape moved again, jerking upright into a ray of dim sunlight.

"Leander?" Dee clutched at her chest. "What are you doing here?"

She was mad at him, right?

Why was she mad at him?

He blinked his amber eyes at her. "I—"

Allie appeared at the top of the stairs, free hand to her head, the cat still gripped in the other.

"What happened last night?" Dee asked, using the bannister to regain her feet, adding a new pain in her tailbone to the list of aches.

They each exchanged wide-eyed stares, clearly one as confused as the other.

"I'm fixing coffee and ... toast, maybe." She could handle coffee and toast. And aspirin. Can't forget the aspirin! "Is it Sunday? It feels like a Sunday."

"Did I sleep in jeans?" Allie asked, dazed.

Somehow, through the cottony softness of her thoughts, Dee didn't think what they'd just come out of was sleep. It felt closer to a horrible rebirth.

She dropped food into Kansas's bowl, her memories completely, conspicuously empty. Something she couldn't remember ever feeling before danced just under her skin, both highlighting each pain point and soothing the ragged edge of her growing anxiety.

Allie dragged herself into the kitchen, also feeding her pet before pulling out a chair and falling into it. "What in the world happened to us?"

Dee looked at her and then to Leander, leaning on the doorframe. "I have no idea."

EPILOGUE

Thump Thump Thump

Ignoring the banging, Theodore turned up the television. On the flatscreen mounted on the wall, a news anchor dressed in a suit wore a grim expression as he announced, "The exonerated suspects Dorseigh Marie McHale and Allison Liddle were key to discovering the real culprit and bringing Leckermaul to justice. Leckermaul awaits trial." The co-anchor with a neat bob next to the anchor nodded along. "The most important thing is that the children have recovered and returned to their families."

"Agreed, Kathy. Also, it seems the exonerated suspects are forming their own private investigation firm."

The coanchor laughed. "They really are Jills of All Trades."

With a derisive snort, Theodore turned off the news. He plumped the final throw pillow before neatly setting it in front of the eleven other throw pillows. He then browsed his closet. Every dress shirt was arranged by sleeve length and then color, whitest white to navy blue. His trousers and suit jackets were all arranged in a similar, orderly manner. Every shoe, tie, hat, and belt were also neatly displayed in a similar manner.

He ignored the section of coveralls bleached so white they were almost luminescent. He owned exactly three, one to commemorate each of them. It was the only thing he allowed himself after it was done, and he was very careful to clean his coveralls thoroughly.

Thump Thump Thump

Black would be more suited to his purpose, but Theodore never wore black. Only those corrupt Catholic priests, Satanists, and social deviants wore black. He would never tarnish his reputation despite the inconvenience. That would tarnish his late wife's reputation, and he would never ever do so.

Thump Thump Thump

Muffled cries followed.

Irritation flooded his nerves as Theodore's gaze swept to the door to the attic. He wanted to wait until after work, after he enjoyed a nice meal at the marina before he took care of *that*, but it seemed he'd have to rearrange the order of which he did things today. Huffing, he went to his bedroom and flipped his late wife's photo on the nightstand to face down. His love didn't need to see or hear what he was about to do.

Thump Thump Thump

Returning to the closet, Theodore carefully removed the suit he was going to wear, folded each article of clothing neatly, and placed them on his dressing chair. Then he removed a coverall from a hanger. After stuffing himself into the coverall, he opened a small drawer filled with shower caps not yet out of the wrapper. He opened one and placed the shower cap over his hair.

The door to the attic swung down. He had long since removed the ladder. One couldn't be too careful with the vermin up there. Theodore jumped and then pulled himself onto the door before clambering all the way onto the attic floor.

AFTERWORD

Deviously Delicious is the first book in the new Jills of All Trades Mystery series. If you enjoyed this book, please leave a review.

ALSO BY BETH WHITEMAN

Forward Yesterday

Who Knew

ALSO BY T.J. DESCHAMPS

MIDLIFE SUPERNATURALS

Eastside Hedge Witch (Book 1)

Eastside Witch Hunt (Book 2)

Eastside Mórrígan (Book 3)

Eastside Coven (Book 4)

Eastside Rock Witch (A Midlife Supernaturals prequel novella) *newsletter signup freebie

Cryptid Essential Oils for Motorcycle Maintenance (A Midlife Supernaturals Novella)

THE ORACLE CHRONICLES

Westside Oracle (Book 1)

Westside Harpy (Book 2)

Westside Titan (Book 3)

Westside Titanomachy (Book 4)

SUPERNATURAL LEGACIES

Wings and Fangs (Book 1) *Fall 2025*

FAERIE TALES SERIES

Ballad of Brave Janet (A Prequel Novella)

Tam Lin (Novella 1)

Warrior Tithe (Novella 2)

Vow Unbroken (Novella 3)

The Formorians (Coming soon)

www.ingramcontent.com/pod-product-compliance
Lightning Source LLC
Chambersburg PA
CBHW030118260626
47156CB00008B/2711